Nice Girls and Other Stories

Nice Girls

and Other Stories

Cezarija Abartis

Printed in Canada.
First Edition
Library of Congress Card Catalog Number: 00-109779
ISBN: 0-89823-215-5
Minnesota Voices Project Number 102, 2003
Book design by Percolator.
Cover: "Flight," detail by Andree Tracey. Courtesy Andree Tracey.

The publication of *Nice Girls and Other Stories* has been made possible by generous grants from the Jerome Foundation, Dayton's Project Imagine with support from the Target Foundation, and the Elmer L. and Eleanor J. Andersen Foundation.

This activity is made possible in part by a grant provided by the Minnesota State Arts Board, through an appropriation by the Minnesota State Legislature. In addition, this activity is supported in part by a grant from the National Endowment for the Arts.

Additional support has been provided by the General Mills Foundation, the McKnight Foundation, the Star Tribune Foundation, and the contributing members of New Rivers Press.

New Rivers Press is a nonprofit literary press associated with Minnesota State University Moorhead.

Wayne Gudmundson, *Director*
Alan Davis, *Senior Editor*
    Managing Editor: Donna Carlson
    Work Study: Charane Wilson
    Honors Apprentice: Robyn Schuricht
    Development Intern: Sandra Arnau-Dewar
    Editorial Interns: Kris Garaas-Johnson, Athena Gracyk, Bret Hoveskeland, Crystal Jensen, Jessie Johnson, Anna Klein, Leslie Knudson, Carrie Olofson, Brett Ortler, Josh Smith, Kristen Tsetsi
Julie Mader-Meersman, *Design and Production Director*
    Design Assistants: Erin Bieri, Renae Brandner, Shannon Tomac
    Photography Assistant: Rachel Broer
    Web Site Development: Daniel Norby, Timothy Litt
        MSUM *Student Technology Team:* John Jeppson, Bo Vargas
Susan Geib, *Marketing Director*
    Marketing Manager: Karen Engelter
Nancy Edmonds Hanson, *Promotion Manager*
Marlane Sanderson, *Business Manager*
    Assistant Business Manager: Andy Peeters

NATIONAL
ENDOWMENT
FOR THE
ARTS

MINNESOTA
STATE ARTS BOARD

New Rivers Press
c/o MSUM
1104 7th Avenue South
Moorhead, MN 56563
www.newriverspress.com

Skiriu mano brangiai šeimai:

To my mother, Cezarija Lapaite Abartis,
and in memory of my father, Peter Abartis (1907-2000)

to Wanda and Bill Green

to Russell Letson

Contents

I

Listen not to vain words of empty tongue.
– Fortune Cookie

"I thought you were a truth seeker," Patrick said.
"Or I suppose I wouldn't have brought it up."
– Ellen Currie, *Moses Supposes*

Homework

I wanted three things in life.

I wanted to be a saint.

I wanted my family to be a normal American family in a *Father Knows Best* house that had a front vestibule with a golden oak stairway to the second floor, wall-to-wall carpeting that I pictured as coral pink on our black-and-white TV, and rooms that were painted rather than wallpapered to conceal the cracks.

The third thing I wanted was Jimmy Osowski, but purely.

I had not seen him for three weeks because I was sick with pneumonia. Finally past the fever and delirium and my parents' terrors, I was in a soft phase of recovery—of pampering, stroking, whimpery tedium.

The windows were steamed over; I was snug under my quilt and the outside world deliciously foggy, invisible. Mother cooked my favorite, cheese dumplings—*kletzku* in Lithuanian—with a sauce of onions sautéed in butter. "Kristina, eat. Be healthy." She brushed the hair out of my eyes. "I make this."

I swallowed down two bites.

"You no want?"

I smiled engagingly.

"I make this."

I shook my head.

"Be strong. Eat." She put a forkful of the glistening dough into her own mouth expectantly. "Maybe you eat later?"

I smiled feebly.

"Poor girl," she said. She rose briskly from the couch I was lying on, slapped her hands together, and said, "Now is time make homework. You want you homework?"

I smiled reluctantly. "Okay."

Mother carried over the small pile of books that had been set on the Motorola. She went to the kitchen, leaving me with my schoolbooks spread out around me, arithmetic, English, and religion. I could hear her clattering among the lunch knives and forks in the sink.

I was in eighth grade at St. Vincent de Paul's. St. Vincent led a life I judged uneventful, only founding an order of priests and laymen. Sure, he was captured by pirates, but he was not one of those martyred in a spectacular fashion after undergoing the supreme test of faith. All the best saints endured a test of chastity or heroic witness. St. Vincent was mostly a good organizer.

The nuns described the lives and exciting deaths of the martyrs. St. Lawrence, for example, was grilled over hot coals! St. Agnes was stabbed in the throat! St. Cecilia's head was chopped nearly completely off! She lived anyway for three days and became the patron saint of musicians.

On the calendar next to the kitchen sink, the saint portrayed for March (*Kovas* in Lithuanian) was St. Joseph in pastels, St. Joseph, the patron of a happy death, presumably in meek old age. In December, though, it would be St. Lucy, in glowing reds and purples, surrounded by a border of braided poinsettias, St. Lucy serenely extending a golden platter with her eyes on it, blue eyes like wet aggies. There were shining blue eyes in her head too, mysteriously restored. The calendar cover was a picture of the sacred heart, on fire and dripping blood. These gift calendars were provided free of charge by a funeral parlor that was owned by two of the Girdis brothers. A third brother owned a flower shop. He belonged to the parish of St. Peter's, his wife's church. St. Peter was given the keys of the kingdom. St. Peter was crucified upside down.

St. Vincent, however, after whom our parish was named, was just a workaday saint. The great days of martyrdom were past.

I picked up my catechism, but it did not hold my attention.

There were two and one-third girls to every boy in St. Vincent de Paul's eighth grade. We eighth-grade girls swooned over Jimmy Osowski, he was so cute.

I imagined what it might be like to kiss Jimmy on the lips. No! Would a saint have such thoughts?

Perhaps I would be one of those saints who reformed after a life of colorful waywardness, but I did not think I could be a great sinner. I did not have the staying power. My sins were venial: talking back to my mother, eating candy during Lent, coveting Mimi Brunowski's poise and angora sweaters.

I rubbed and rubbed my lips.

Mother walked in from the kitchen, drying her hands. "Want Chapstick?" she asked.

"No." I wanted Jimmy Osowski to bring me my homework assignment.

Mother went to the window and stood there, gazing across the street, her feet wide apart and solid like a wrestler sizing up an opponent. Sighing, she turned to the corner cupboard and got out her bag of knitting (it was a brown cap for me). She looked at me and clucked sympathetically. She bent over to kiss me on the top of the head. I could hear Father stamping his boots on the doormat outside the kitchen door. When he came into the living room, she said, "Big shot late. Take off you boots."

My father—tall and a little stooped—smiled anxiously, guiltily, as if it should be he and not I who was suffering.

She stalked out of the room past Father, who leaned against the wall and slowly removed his boots, holding one in each hand so it would not tap against the other and drop snow. A clump had already melted and made a dark, heart-shaped spot on the carpet's pattern of brown plumes. When Mother returned she stared at the wet stain, pulled a cleaning rag out of her apron pocket, and silently got down on her knees to pat the carpet dry.

Then she gave me my medicine even though it was early. Father watched me take it bravely and followed Mother into the kitchen.

I liked the mud-colored cough syrup, sharp and hot at the back of my throat. I did not mind the Vick's Vaporub, pungent in my nostrils and on my chest, or the cotton scarf wrapped around my neck, fastened by a safety pin. The only price to pay was the chicken soup with carrots and slimy celery and the sticky drink of warm milk with raw egg and honey in it.

I hoped to be well by Easter so I could march in the eighth-grade girls' procession. The church was wood frame and held perhaps one hundred pews, but it felt large and mystic. I curled up under my blanket and thought of the rich, smoky, tickling incense and Latin hymns *(Pange lingua glori-oh-oh-si)* thickening the air, the perfumed thread of voices ascending, spiraling, and embracing.

Heaven would be like that, I thought. In heaven my name would be Stella, not Kristina; I was toying with that name for myself. I would be the first saint named Stella.

Even in early spring in Pittsburgh, we would wear white dresses with puffs of short sleeves for the procession and hang up our winter coats and gloves in the dank basement where we assembled. Released from sturdy winter cloth, we would cradle our elbows in our cupped hands and shiver.

But once we were in the holy atmosphere we would not be cold, as the organ music surged behind us from the choir loft and we were caught up, lifted forward toward the altar, almost floating in our organdy dresses and white anklets.

I imagined myself passing Jimmy Osowski in a pew beside his parents and watching them out of the corner of my eye. His mother looked American—trim and petite. My mother was short and blocky. Jimmy's father was not as handsome nor as tall as my father, but he was wearing a sedate navy-blue suit and white shirt. My father was wearing a yellow shirt, gray Orlon cardigan, and a dark green jacket over that.

My father worked at Federal Enamel and Paint Company, a factory that put the white, or sometimes speckled, enamel coat on pots and pans. We never lacked for chipped basins and roasters and saucepans; we got to buy the seconds at a discount. I would have preferred him to work in a navy-blue jacket and tie, to be in insurance, to give people security.

Just before I got sick, I had been to the optometrist and ordered a new pair of glasses, *cat's-eye* glasses, the latest style, and now I fretted about them. My parents were unable to comprehend my nearsightedness. Neither of them wore glasses; they came of good stock, how could I need glasses?

But they accepted this American deficiency in me, induced by watching too much television and reading too many books, too many words in the American language.

I yearned for my new cat's-eye glasses so that I would be pretty when Jimmy brought my assignment from school. At least I hoped Jimmy would be the one.

My father had finally picked up my glasses that morning. I was trying to get used to the new prescription. When I put them on, everything was clean and geometric through the center of the lenses, but at the thick edges, the world was still blurred and rubbery, which took getting used to. Nevertheless, I liked looking at the solid couch, the brown carpet, the cold bright day outside, the orderliness of the dominoes Mother and I had between us.

"How my princess?" my father asked. He was out of breath and red-faced. He had just returned from helping our neighbor, Mrs. Gallent. Her battery was dead.

The green of his jacket looked very green and piercing. As I swiveled my head, he rippled and contracted at the periphery of my lenses.

Mother glared at him and loudly clapped together the leaves of the board game we had been playing earlier. She raked the Old Maid cards into the package and put away the Sorry game. She accidentally brushed against a domino piece; I replaced it in its position.

"How my princess?" he repeated.

7

"Fine," I said. I wiggled the frames to fit more closely.

"I love you," he said. He looked uneasy.

"It's not your fault I'm sick. Anyway, I'm almost well." I gave a small cough and covered my mouth in a refined way.

Sheepishly he patted my hand, then went into the kitchen and packed his bologna sandwich in a paper bag to take to work, the afternoon shift.

"No be late today," my mother shouted after him. "Buy quart of milk for my sick girl."

More lukewarm eggnog.

Our neighbor across the street, Mrs. Gallent, was beautiful. She had platinum hair, slim hips, and long legs. In the summertime, like a movie star, she wore a two-piece scarlet bathing suit for suntanning in the backyard. She wobbled out in her high-heeled slippers, positioned a beach towel on the slanted cellar door, and lay in the afternoon sun for hours. She placed little spoon-shaped plastic covers over her eyes to protect them; at other times she put on sunglasses with pink cat's-eye frames. Her husband had a good job as a driver for Acme Family Movers. He wore a large-brimmed cowboy hat even when he was not working.

The one time I saw her in our house was when I first came down with pneumonia. She knocked on the door as Mother was lacing her thick-soled oxfords to trudge to her job in the hospital laundry. Mrs. Gallent swept in wearing a flared, tight-waisted crimson coat and held out a glass jar. "Mrs. Astrauskas, I prepared some homemade chicken soup for your Kristina. I hear she's sick, poor child."

"How you know she sick?" Mother's mouth was a squeezed line.

I was embarrassed at her peasant suspicion. "Thank you, Mrs. Gallent," I piped. "How kind of you."

Mrs. Gallent seemed relieved by my perfect manners. "And I brought some Hershey bars too," she said as she winked at me. "We can't be saints every minute of the day." Her voice tinkled.

She turned and moved like a blond ballerina on a music box. She seemed fluffy and light compared to my squat, stolid, brown-haired mother.

"Thank you very much, Mrs. Gallent," I said, hoping my voice tinkled.

"Thank you," Mother said firmly.

Mrs. Gallent looked around and cleared her throat in a delicate way. "I can see I came at a busy time. You're about to go out." She lifted one pale pink, manicured hand, encircled by a clinking charm bracelet, waved daintily, and fluttered out. The door clicked shut. Her perfume lingered in the winter air.

"I can pay for chocolate candy by myself," Mother said under her breath. "I know how make soup."

"It was only a gesture, Mother. A neighborly gesture of goodwill."

"What is 'gesture'?"

"A good deed, something good."

"Is good she sleep in sun with no clothes?"

"Mother." I rolled my eyes up to the ceiling. "She was wearing a bathing suit."

"All afternoon with no clothes. She should be working in house, cleaning house like good wife."

"I bet her house *is* clean."

"Hah, look at her windows! Dirty, dirty, dirty."

"Mother, it's the end of winter. They get dirty in winter."

"*My* windows clean."

The next afternoon Sister Mary Augustine telephoned, saying in her tiny, holy voice she would send someone with my assignment. I began to look forward to seeing Jimmy Osowski. I knew it would not be Taffy because she was home with the flu, and Verna, my second-best friend, lived in the opposite direction. I put my palms together and prayed to the Blessed Virgin Mother to let it be Jimmy Osowski.

Surely Jimmy Osowski would think differently about me in my new glasses. Surely he would think me pretty in my gray slanty *cat's-eye* glasses. Maybe even beautiful.

I longed for Jimmy Osowski with a longing previously reserved for heaven. Dear God, let Jimmy admire my new glasses.

"Is cold here," Mother said as she paced in front of the window. I was on the couch in the living room, my books scattered around me. She turned away from the window and shivered. "You pretty." She brought her beige flannel housecoat to drape over my shoulders.

The beige robe hung limply from her outstretched arm. She was colorless, stocky, unrefined. Did I resemble her? "I don't want it." I clamped my lips and picked up the book closest to hand.

"You shamed of me."

"What time is Dad coming home?"

"You love him more. I work hard for you. I work every day, and you love him more."

I defied her. I opened up *Ivanhoe,* which was in my lap.

She let the robe drop. It fell on the couch with the hem dragging on the floor. "You hurt you eyes. You read too much." Her hand was clenched at her side. She took a harsh breath and walked stiffly out of the room.

I thrummed my fingers on the open book. I did not feel like reading. Ivanhoe loved the fair Rowena. Could I be said to be fair? At least I had blond hair. Well, brownish-blond. I craned my neck to see my reflection in the window across the room, but I could not. Rising from the couch, I kicked the robe aside. Outdoors the ground was bare and bleak without the sparkling, soft snow cover. Across the street, where Mrs. Gallent lived and next to her, Mr. and Mrs. Valko, in the shadowed spaces under the trees and by the cellars of the houses the snow was rotting—brown ice mixed with gravel and sand and, for all I knew, dog turds. I turned away, to the closed-up fireplace. At either end of the mantel was a fake flowerpot with red paper roses, and in the middle was a glass bowl in the shape of a hand holding wooden apples and bananas, and beside it a pink porcelain ballerina on one pointed toe. I focused on the mirror behind the knickknacks. I stuck my tongue out at the ghostly brat.

I snapped on the television and watched *Queen for a Day*. The winning contestant received a beautiful Maytag washer. Dimples appeared in her beaming face.

There was a knock on the door at three-thirty, just after the last class, P.O.D. (Problems of Democracy—twice a week). Mother opened the door.

It was Louie Brunelli.

Nobody liked him, he had cooties. He was pudgy, greasy-haired, and wore wool trousers. He didn't live in our neighborhood. He laid the books and sheets down on the spindle-back chair and slowly unwound his homemade muffler, swaying and grunting where its extra length was tangled.

"How come *you're* bringing me my assignment?"

He lifted his plump shoulders in puzzlement and scratched his round head.

"I mean, you don't live in the neighborhood."

"Sister Mary Augustine asked for volunteers."

"Nobody else volunteered?"

"I wanted to help Sister Mary Augustine."

I sank down under the covers. So much for my friends. They didn't like me. They probably thought I had cooties. "Have we finished *Ivanhoe*?"

"Almost."

"How far are we?"

"She wrote it down, Sister Mary Augustine. I don't like it. Too many hard words."

He showed me where the class was in arithmetic, P.O.D., science; he told me what they had done in art and music, how much they had memorized of the Baltimore catechism.

I watched him as he poked through his notes with his short

fingers, as he sniffled, as he pushed his glasses up on his snub nose, as a sheen of sweat rose on his upper lip where some darker hairs were sprouting. "How's Jimmy?" I asked.

"Jim Woycek?"

"Jimmy Osowski." I liked even the way his name filled my mouth.

"Okay."

"He's not sick?"

"Huh?"

"Oh, sick with the flu?" I said casually. I must have sounded like his mother questioning him about earmuffs or clean socks.

"No." He shifted in the chair. Maybe he did have cooties.

"A lot of the kids have flu is why I asked."

He yawned. "Gotta go," he said, standing up. "Mom made butterscotch cake."

"Will someone else bring my homework next week?"

Louie shrugged.

"Will it be you?"

"I don't know." He buttoned his jacket unevenly and had to start all over again. "Maybe. I don't mind."

Mother came in as he left. "Nice boy," she said. "Do his parents go in our church?"

"I don't know. I guess." I was sullen.

"You no feel good?"

"I feel fine. I'm fine."

The next morning I dropped my glasses and broke a lens. Mother sighed and clamped her lips. Father quickly offered, "I take glasses in doctor." He left almost immediately, and when he returned at lunchtime, he reported that the lens would be replaced pretty soon.

That day I wore my old tortoiseshell glasses and read *Ivanhoe,* but I was getting dizzy and woozy from the old prescription. The words squirmed before my eyes. Mother tired of my complaining and telephoned Dr. Horwitz.

The call took a long while. When she returned she was silent and her face was washed pale, like St. Joseph on the kitchen calendar. She marched to the window, yanked the lace curtain open, and stared across the street. An oily yellow sunlight seeped in.

"Mother?"

"What you want?"

I was impatient. "When will my glasses be fixed?"

"Soon. When no-good big shot go in doctor."

"Will I have them next week? I'll have new homework next week."

"Do hooligan bring it?"

"I thought you liked Louie Brunelli."

She pinched the curtains closed. The light in the room became thin and milky again.

I persisted. "Will I have my glasses next week?"

"Soon." She wheeled around and stomped into the kitchen.

I clicked on the television and watched *Search for Tomorrow,* which my mother mispronounced as "Church for Tomorrow." The wife, Ann Taylor, blond and long-suffering, was reunited with her husband after his brief fling with his secretary, Ramona. She embraced him and forgave him. In the background there was organ music rippling, at first benevolently, then triumphantly. The husband bought her a dozen white long-stemmed real roses. In the last segment the mother, the father, and their two children were smilingly sitting at the dinner table, eating what looked like tunafish casserole.

I decided to make peace with Mother. "Mother, let's watch television together," I yelled toward the kitchen. "Keep me company."

She shuffled in with tears running down her cheeks.

"Mama, why are you crying?" I sat up, gripping the blanket hard.

"Nothing." She wiped her tears with the back of her wrist. Her eyes glittered like St. Lucy's.

"I'm getting better. Look, I'm almost well." I opened my

mouth wide for her to check my throat.

"I know."

"Why are you crying?"

"Holy Mary not listen my prayer." She plucked at her apron pocket, pulled out a tissue and began to shred it. "You no love me. You father no love me."

I put my arms around her and stroked her shoulders and back as she gave great, heaving sobs. "I'm sorry I lost my temper. I do love you." She sobbed implacably. I clung to her.

Gradually her sobbing subsided; she moved out of my arms and leaned against the couch, exhausted. We sat in front of the Motorola and watched *Days of Our Lives* and *Guiding Light*. She brought out her brown bag of handwork. She began to knit furiously.

I dozed off toward the end of *Guiding Light* and had unrestful dreams about my parents, about tugging against my mother, about Jimmy.

"She no good, she garbage!" my mother screamed at my father in the kitchen. That was not part of a dream. Mother really was yelling.

I withered. How could I betray my parents this way? How could I be garbage? I saw my heavenly crown flapping away from me on angel wings. I was glad that Jimmy Osowski was not there to hear of my guilt.

I saw the turquoise and gold gates of heaven shut. I heard the lock snap. Jimmy Osowski would go to heaven, but not me. I would be forever closed out when even my parents found me repugnant.

"She *not* bad." My father defended me.

"Shut up," she cried. "Shut up."

"She no want trouble."

"Sonofabitch," my mother yelled.

I made a tent of the top blankets and tunneled underneath, but I could still hear them.

"It no her fault," my father persisted.

I promised God I would never lust again.

"*Rupuže!*"

I was hurt. My mother had never called me a toad before.

Maybe God was giving me a trial. I would relinquish Jimmy Osowski and all thoughts of him. I would become pure. I would, when I grew up, become a Bride of Christ, join some cloistered order where the nuns did not speak but ate cold gruel and wore hair shirts under their long, white garments. I twitched.

No. I could not do it.

I still wanted Jimmy Osowski to bring me my homework next week. I could not wipe out thoughts of him, his cute eyes and manly mouth. I would exchange a crown in heaven for Jimmy bringing my books.

"Why you do this? You lie about doctor. You no go in doctor. You go in her house."

Maybe it was not me my father was defending. Mother said *you*. I heard a dish roll and crash.

"*Rupuže!* Sonofabitch Mrs. Gallent! You no big shot. You big shit. You want my blood. You want kill me. I cut you heart. I cut *my* heart."

I heard a drawer screech open and cutlery rattle.

"Blood! You want blood!" Her voice ascended a ladder of shrieks, higher and higher. "I cut my heart."

I put my fists over my ears, but I could still hear with the inside of my skin. I burned.

"Stop!" he shouted. "No!"

I heard stumbling, a chair clatter to the floor, flesh thump dully against the wall, metal skip and skitter across the tiles.

In the living room, where I shivered under my tent of blankets I saw, against the light and through the weave of the blanket, her form stumble in and sway between the doorjambs. I slowly lifted my head out from under the covers. Her apron was spattered with blood. I did not understand such red against so glaring a white apron. At the top a crimson stain dribbled an eerie upside-down crown.

She clutched her left hand in her right, and blood seeped out between her fingers. She must have cut her hand. I would never lust again if only God would restore her fingers.

Father appeared and, facing her, gently put his hands on her shoulders. "I take in doctor." His mournful tone asked for permission. "Doctor fix."

They both floated before me in the doorway, and I felt the living room couch fall from under my body: her blood, as in the calendar pictures of the martyrs, spouted from her hand in banners, rolled down his trouser legs, down to the carpet, and up into the atmosphere of the room, dyeing it in a red fog, pervading the air with the smell of wet copper and salt.

I pushed myself up on my elbows, the blankets sliding away in the oddly chill air. My heart was pounding and hot. I blinked and squinted. Slowly Mother and Father descended to the floor. She was still holding her hand. He grasped her elbow and pulled her toward the kitchen. She shook him off.

"Go in hell," Mother said, chin down on her chest. She leaned against the doorway and breathed slowly, heavily. She dabbed at her face with her unhurt hand. "I need Band-Aid."

There really was not much blood, a few spots that had frightened me. The apron was embroidered with little nosegays of flowers in a band across the bottom. No dribbles and shadows of blood, just pinprick vivid drops. I had been mistaken about the fingers sliced through.

Her face was splotched. "It was accident," she said, noticing me, her eyes glittering, full. "Sorry."

I pulled the covers up to my chest. I cleared my throat, as if I were going to speak. I cleared my throat again.

"Sorry," she said, walking away from me into the kitchen.

"Sorry," he said. He turned and followed her. His shoulders slumped. "Sorry."

I heard them clumping up the stairs, heard water run in the bathroom sink.

I took a deep breath very quietly. A cough was prowling inside my chest. It seemed to coil inside my ribs around my heart. It scrambled to get out, but I clamped my mouth shut. I picked up my book, which had slipped to the floor. When I held the book at arm's length at a certain angle, the sun reflected off the plastic cover and shone in my eyes so that I could not see.

New Girl

In the buzzing school cafeteria, with its murky brown wall tiles and steamy smell, I found myself sitting at a table with this slow girl. She wore a mushroom-colored dress. She was in the eighth grade too, I thought.

I had Tuesday's usual, chicken à la king. Hilda, three chairs over, warily unwrapped a baloney-and-lettuce sandwich from home. I could hear her liquid chewing. Her face was large and framed by limp, yellowish hair; she had short, pale lashes and little eyes squeezed between her bony brows and cheeks.

I thought of myself as an improver. A scolder, a fixer, a patter-and-puller. Hilda Grace Meyers became my project.

I had broken up with my best friend, Trixie. Her big brother was a Marine, and he had won a medal in Korea. Their house had two bathrooms, and she and her sister had separate bedrooms. Trixie's smooth lift of silver-blond hair ended in a flip, while mine was flat and dull light brown. At that very moment Trixie sat beside Alice a few tables away.

Trixie had made fun of a boy I said was cute. I became more and more angry and called the boy she had a crush on "Big Ears" and "Dummy" because he had flunked a grade.

That was last week. Today, I wanted to make up with her. Trixie's navy blue dress with its white collar of crocheted rosettes was my favorite. She always wore nylons with this outfit whereas I was allowed to wear nylons only on Sunday to church. She delicately lifted out a portion of her chicken à la king and placed it on Alice's plate. Alice giggled gratefully.

I turned back to the girl chewing loosely down the table. "Hi, my name's Juliet," I said to Hilda.

Hilda cast her eyes in my direction, then looked down. "Hi."

At first I thought I recognized her from my English class, where we were reading *Silas Marner*, which our teacher said was about finding your real treasure, but no, that was an accelerated class, Hilda wasn't in that. It was Mrs. Yost's science class I had seen her in. We were studying earthworms and species. Hilda sat in the last row.

She had transferred to our school at the beginning of the year, when her family left their farm. Hilda told me about the farm. She knew how to tie sailor's knots and pick dry weeds and could search inside a chicken for the pink clusters of half-formed eggs.

Then Hilda and I discussed parasites. That seemed even worse. She told me how their pigs used to have parasites; their cows, too. I thought about it. Having things grow INSIDE you! And these things were around you all the time! Even in the food you ate! Like in pork. This was in addition to all the germs you could not see with the naked eye.

Hilda was philosophical. "I don't mind doing cleaning sometimes."

I turned around and saw Trixie and Alice bend their heads together and snicker intimately. Trixie's silver cloud of hair trembled and shook and seemed to flash in the muddy light.

I moved over next to Hilda. She chewed her baloney-and-lettuce sandwich with her lips half-parted as she stammered, "I don't . . . don't get . . . don't understand fractions." There was a speck of lettuce on the corner of her upper lip.

"It's simple," I said, impatient with her slow and messy chewing, for I was raised politely. "Anybody can do that."

She fixed her wet eyes on me. "Maybe so, but *I* can't."

I watched Trixie, five tables away, bumping her shoulder against Alice. Trixie and Alice started to slap each other's hands playfully with their fingertips. Then Trixie hugged Alice and began to fool with her hair, patting it, winding it on her finger, filling it out. Trixie was wearing a ring that glittered and dazzled in the smeary air.

I glanced at Hilda's chunky and yellowish hands. "All right. I'll show you after school." Hilda said nothing, not thank you, not even a smile. "You should wipe your mouth. There's a piece of food."

Slowly she rubbed her mouth with her open hand.

"It's still there. Use your napkin."

"Okay now?"

I nodded apathetically. I stabbed at my chicken lumps, lackadaisically chasing them around the plate. "Want a taste?"

"I don't care," Hilda said. She was not pretty, not appealing, not smart; yet out of this unmoving set of qualities came an indifference to the act of pleasing that I envied, that I found prideful, almost irresistible.

I cut off a corner of burned toast and chicken à la king and slid my plate over to her. "Well, I can meet you after school."

She stared at the beige flour-and-chicken paste that was congealing on the toast. "What time should I be ready?"

"You can come to my homeroom just after class."

Hilda crumpled the waxed paper from her sandwich and brushed off the table. "Okay," she said. "I have to see Mr. Beymer now before class. I need extra help." She squinted at me, smiled, and picked up her books in one hand and my plate and crumpled paper in the other to take over to the stacks of trays and dirty dishes. "Bye." The plate had left a moist ring.

She carried the books tightly and, turning sideways, making herself smaller, squeezed between the tables. When she got past the outer row of tables she strode along, taking loose-jointed, awkwardly hanging steps. Her clothes seemed to hang on her lanky body; her straw-colored hair seemed to hang lanky too.

I snuck a peek over in Trixie and Alice's direction. They were already gone. I sat alone until the buzzer sounded for afternoon classes.

In our science class, Mrs. Yost explained that it was crucial to study our lessons. The Russians had already beat us with their *Sputnik*. The United States needed scientists and engineers for the space program, and our scientists were working as hard as they could. I agreed. I would go to college, I would major in science, I would save us. I did not know then that in just a few months, our own *Explorer* would be launched into the airless, soundless dark of space, where it would stay for twelve years, surpassing *Sputnik*'s ninety-two days. And so, our American scientists proved to be superior. I did not have to be concerned. I was always better in English anyway.

In the back row, Hilda stared with soft eyes at the window, holding her chin in her hand. The wind outside was rising; the weather was changing; there would be rain or maybe snow tomorrow. A few yellow leaves still clung to the swaying boughs. Hilda's lips twitched and her eyes narrowed; she seemed to be thinking but I did not know what, could not imagine what.

"Juliet, I was asking you a question," Mrs. Yost said. "Pay attention."

"Yes, Mrs. Yost." I looked toward Hilda, who looked at me. Mrs. Yost should have scolded *her*.

I waited in my homeroom. Our teacher was nice and allowed us to put up sports pennants supporting our Pittsburgh Pirates, though they didn't make it to the World Series in 1957. The black-and-gold pennants were pinned next to cutouts of Halloween pumpkins on the bulletin board. I did not follow sports much; I preferred books, movies, fashion magazines, and the poetry that our teacher taught us—the poetry of Elinor Wylie, Francis X. Thompson, Longfellow, Edgar Allan Poe—but it was nice of her to let us express our interests, and I tried to imitate her. So I worked with this slow, lumbering girl even though she was not in our class. "Like this, Hilda. This is the right way to do it. Put the number here."

"Okay." She made a faint, uncertain, wavy mark on the paper.

"No, no, that's all wrong. Like this. Like THIS."

"Okay." She made a mark beside her previous one.

"I told you that's wrong, Hilda, wrong."

She brushed a strand of pale hair behind her ear and I saw she had fawn-like ears, pointy ears. I congratulated myself for not making fun of her ears.

"Sometimes I think you're a cipher, Hilda. I'll tell you what that is."

"I know what a cipher . . ." She took a deep breath and swallowed. "Cipher is," she repeated. "My father calls me stupid when he gets mad. I don't like it." Her eyes filled. "My brother is being sent overseas in the army. I wish I could show you on a map." She rubbed her eyes so they became swollen and pink, eyes that looked as if they belonged to an insignificant, squeaking creature.

I thought she was going to cry, but she did not. "I'm sorry. Let's work on this later. You study hard and we'll work on this tomorrow."

I strolled home past the store windows painted with Halloween scenes. On the front window of Dietz's Flower Shoppe was painted a silhouette of a witch flying on a broom; Miller's Men's Store had puffy cartoon ghosts with surprised round eyes, not actually frightening, not like the real ghosts in dreams. I could paint much better scenes than a yellow moon shining on a skinny cat or a ghost in a bedsheet. The wind blew loose papers down the street. I sauntered past Grogan's Real Estate, the A & P Grocery, Haser's Funeral Home; of course, that did not have decorated windows. I walked to the movie theater and studied the glossies of the film showing at the Orpheum, *The Spirit of St. Louis,* a movie about airplanes. Their movies were never as good as the movies which cost ten cents more at the Roxian in the next block, where *Gunfight at the O.K. Corral* was playing.

That night I had a dream. There were lobsters splashing in a pot on the stove and chickens roasting in the oven. I had never tasted lobster; the only thing I knew about them was that they became red as they were boiled alive. These lobsters gave off high-pitched squeals. The chickens too tried to claw their way out of the oven, but I hurled stones at the oven door.

When I whirled around to escape, I nearly dropped into a chasm. On the other side of the chasm, Hilda, tall, bony, and with wings, popped up. I hefted a jagged rock in my palm, turning it and feeling the sharp points.

She bent her knees slightly and began to flap her wings, slowly, and then deeply to gain momentum.

At my feet there were plops and snicks; there was a whizzing next to my cheek. From across the chasm, someone was flinging rocks at me.

I woke up, my heart beating.

Cold, blue light slashed across the bedroom ceiling as the curtains stirred. In the dark the shadows of the dresser and chair looked like hills. Sleeping peacefully in her bed against the wall, my sister gave off soft, regular sighs.

After school the following day Hilda and I found an empty classroom. She brought me an oatmeal raisin cookie and an oak leaf, perfectly flat and bronze-colored, which I did not need nor want. "Thanks."

"It's pretty," she said. "Different."

"I guess." To me it looked like every other fallen leaf on the slick ground. The radiator hissed. Outside, the rain was being driven in a slant by the fierce wind. It ticked like a clock or like pebbles thrown against the window.

"Want this cookie?"

"No thanks, I don't care for oatmeal."

She slipped it back into her paper sack. The leaf lay between us at the edge of her desk. She pressed the leaf with her thick fingers. "I flunked my test." She flattened the already-flat leaf against the nicked and ink-stained desktop. "S. loves Don" was carved inside a wobbly heart.

"Don't worry about it. It's just one test. You'll pass the next one." Trixie walked by the doorway, her head high in the air. She was wearing her beige cashmere sweater. "Mrs. Exeter likes you," I offered. "You'll be all right."

"You really think so?"

I looked away and nodded. A low branch with a few yellow leaves stuck on it clicked against the window, knocking, knocking, scratching at the glass.

"I'd like to be smart like you, Juliet. I wish I was smart. I wish I knew things. I wish I could spell." She said this in a small voice.

I felt warm and happy and pretty. "Maybe if you keep trying."

"It won't happen. I'm dumb as they come."

"You're not."

"Everybody says so. I know it." She locked her hands in her lap.

"We'll work on this tomorrow." I stacked my green geography book on top of my blue history book and neatened the edges.

"I wish I was smart like you. You don't have to work hard."

I teased out a strand of hair and spiraled it around my finger. I had skipped a year in school. "On some things I do."

"Not like me."

I thought about it. "I have to practice my piano." I stretched out my fingers to admire them. "And I memorize dates for my history test."

She swallowed hard. "It's not the same."

I relished her compliments.

Be kind to those less fortunate, Mother taught us. "Why don't you invite Hilda Grace for dinner sometime." She had long hair for a mother, hair that touched her shoulders, but she usually wore it loosely pulled back in a rubber band. She looked like an older sister or cousin, not a mother. I was proud of her youth and beauty, and I wished she wore expensive gauzy dresses. She had wanted to go to college, the University of Pittsburgh, to study art history, but she married Father right after high school.

"Invite Hilda Grace over sometime. She seems a nice girl. Do you like her?"

"She's okay." I passed the au gratin potatoes to Frankie, who looked at me sideways with slitted eyes. I complained to an unhearing world, "Why do we always have potatoes all rotten?"

"I *love* potatoes au gratin," Frankie said and spooned out a large portion.

Mother passed the chicken in a sauce of canned mushroom soup, smiling widely, as if it were a treat. "Hilda Grace is new this year, isn't she?"

"I guess."

Mother got up to turn on the radio. She dialed the knob through crackle and static and found the station she wanted. The commercial for fifty beautiful moments of the classical piano had ended, and the evening news came on with an announcement that *Sputnik,* which had been launched on October fourth, was still orbiting the earth, crossing the United States seven times a day; it was expected to orbit for a number of years. Mother stared at Father and sighed. Frankie and I kicked each other's toes under the table. The announcer continued more brightly with the news that the Public Health Service said that the number of cases of polio was decreasing by two-thirds, especially paralytic cases. Salk developed his vaccine at the University of Pittsburgh. We were winning.

Dad helped himself to chicken. It was one of his favorites, along with meatloaf, which he liked because he could take cold meatloaf sandwiches to the plant the next day. "You might want to introduce this girl to your other friends."

"Do your other friends like her?" Mother said this with an expectation high in her voice.

I did not relieve her. "Doubt it."

"What difference does it make as long as Juliet likes her?"

"That's not what I meant, Cyrus."

Dad did not reply, as though he had been justly scolded. The broccoli steamed in front of Mother. Her tight forehead glistened with perspiration. The sleeves of her turquoise blouse were rolled up to the elbows. She had slender arms. She rubbed her forehead and glanced outside anxiously. It was a gray, indistinct October twilight that looked thick and webbed even though it was only five-thirty. Then her eyes slid indoors to scan the walls. I disapproved of the wallpaper Mother had chosen, with its gaudy daffodils and violets illogically the same size as the collie dogs apparently frolicking and leaping out of the garden. Her eyes moved to where we four, with our chipped dishes, sat around the large, ill-proportioned dining room table handed down from her mother. The table had bulbous legs that flared out at the bottom to trip a person.

With a nasty smile pasted on her face, Frankie handed me the chicken. "Why don't you like Hilda Grace?" Was she mimicking Mother? She stretched out Hilda's name.

"It's her voice." I thought Frankie's eyes twinkled. The dimples in her cheeks made me want to smack her.

"What about it?" Mother put a bite of potatoes in her mouth.

"She stammers sometimes."

"She's probably uneasy." Mother glided over difficulties.

"Well, I don't like it. She's been asking me to help her. She sounds stupid. I don't like the sound of her voice."

"But Hilda Grace likes you?" Mother asked, forcing a smooth tone.

"Retards always like Jule and Jule likes retards." Frankie grinned wickedly. "Just kidding."

"That's not funny," Dad said. "That's not the way we talk around here. You could hurt someone's feelings."

"Jule doesn't have any feelings," Frankie said. "She's iron, cast iron."

Mother set her knife down on the plate. "Why are you two jumping at each other? What has gotten into you two?"

"Maybe it's Jule's period."

I had kept virtuously quiet, but even my virtue had a limit. "You little brat. You stupid, snotty brat. You're spoiling for a

Nice Girls and Other Stories

beating." She stuck her tongue out at me. My patience broke.
"You stupid worm, you toad, you creepy bug."

"Stinker."

"Queer."

"Toadsucker."

Father stood up. "Enough. One more word and both of you
are staying home this weekend." He was short but nobody would
have described him that way because he had such a quiet, upward
presence, as though he were sure of himself and sure of how others
would receive him.

Frankie and I scrutinized our plates. My chicken supreme
lay under its mushroom-flecked sauce; opposite it sat the khaki-
colored broccoli; my cheesy potatoes mocked me oozingly.

For a while there was just the clinking of silverware. Then
Mother said, "What have I forgotten?" She surveyed the table and
tapped it a few times with her fingertips. She pushed the three
serving bowls into the exact center so they touched. "I've forgotten
something." In the kitchen the clock ticked. "The rolls. They're in
the oven."

They were burned. She glanced at my plate and frowned. "If
you don't finish your chicken, you won't get any apple crisp."

Frankie grinned at me.

I emitted a small, pitiful cough.

Mother leaned forward and felt my forehead. "You're not
feeling well? Are you sick? How is your stomach?"

"I'm all right, I think." I smiled weakly. "I guess I'm not hungry. Do I have to finish the chicken?"

"No," Mother said and at the same time Father said, "It's
good food. We shouldn't coddle her."

I ate one bite of the potatoes. I ate one bite of chicken. I ate
one bite of broccoli. Mother spooned out the apple crisp and I
got my share.

Frankie held up her dessert bowl. "In my class too there's
kind of a dopey girl that nobody likes. She weighs about two hundred pounds. Named Betsy Collins." Frankie had just received

straight A's on her report card. I got one B but it was in Phys. Ed.

I intended to admonish Frankie; she needed it. "You're re-pulsive to judge people that way. You ought to be ashamed of such ignorant behavior."

Father heaved a sigh. "I've just about had it with you two."

"I was only saying Betsy in my class is not popular too. She's not well-liked."

"Who cares if she's well-liked." Finally, Father was rebuking Frankie, as she richly deserved.

"There is nothing wrong with being popular, being well-liked." Mother was loving and temperamental. She could be rash and then regretful and mopey. But this time it was Father who snapped.

He closed his eyes for a second and said levelly, "Marge, you sound like *Death of a Salesman*."

"I don't care if I do sound like one of your stupid, precious books."

I corrected her. "It's not a stupid book. It's a stupid play by Arthur Miller."

She swiveled toward me and slapped me, but because she was sitting at my side the slap was awkward, glanced off my jaw. Or maybe she restrained herself at the last minute. I was not hurt so much as surprised and humiliated. My mother was not a person to hit for punishment.

She pushed her chair away from the table so hard it banged against the table leg and thumped to the floor. "I wanted a quiet meal, something elegant for once. Is that so much to ask?" She stamped out.

Father stood up and went after her, and Frankie and I were left in the kitchen alone. She shoved her apple slices around in the bowl. Her shoulders slumped. "See what you started," I said.

"You did it," she said, but not very quickly, not with conviction.

Father came back into the kitchen and sighed. "Your mother is having a hard time right now because of her sister's troubles. You have to be extra nice. She has a lot of things on her mind."

"I'm sorry, Dad," Frankie said.

"I'll help around the house," I said.

"Your mother is not herself," Father said softly and without accusation.

I would understand this better in years to come, when I myself was not to be myself.

My mother was on edge because her younger sister was pregnant with their second child and her husband, Tad, a gambler and good-for-nothing sponger, had enlisted in the army. "Now of all times," Mother had said. "What a fool, what a useless fool to imagine he can run away."

In church on the Sunday before All Saints' Day and All Souls' Day, Father Connelly reminded us that we should pray for the souls in Purgatory, for the souls who longed for liberation and heaven as their sins burned away. At Saturday afternoon confession, I had confessed my disobedience and my swearing (I had called Frankie a "creepy bug," which was not exactly profanity but I didn't want to provoke a fight). Father Connelly sighed, gave me my penance of five Hail Marys, and uttered his ritual farewell, "Go and sin no more." But I always did. I thought about the stars and planets and now the lone Russian satellite orbiting above us. The satellite traveled at eighteen thousand miles per hour; it circled the globe every ninety-six minutes; the satellite would continue to send radio signals from space to the Earth until it fell into the atmosphere and burned up. A few years later we were able to see photographs from space: the Earth floats like a blue-green pearl against the plushy night, self-enclosed and serene. I studied the statue of Mary in her sky-blue mantel at the front, with her mild, unreadable face, her arms spread in invitation to the faithful but perhaps to the unfaithful too. I thought about how we were all souls yearning for light and love. I felt bad for Hilda, who was lonely. I felt guilty for those who were treating her uncharitably. I bent forward and saw Trixie sitting next to Alice in the pew across the aisle. Often Trixie went to the noon Mass while her parents went at ten o'clock. Hilda did not go to the Catholic church. She was Lutheran. I liked our church. The choir sang in Latin. The hymn was about God's glory and love. But Lutherans were pretty good, too.

⋕ ⋕ ⋕ ⋕

Invite her, Mother had told me. Later in the week Hilda smiled and said she would ask permission. She glided down the hall, stumbling once but catching herself against the wall, and turned into Mrs. Exeter's room. Trixie and Alice strolled past. They were conversing with one another and I heard "Stupid" and "Nutty." Alice glanced at me and twirled her index finger at her temple; Trixie burst out in laughter, covering her mouth with her free hand. She had a charm bracelet of gold animals around her wrist. They dangled and jingled. Trixie and Alice turned at the end of the hall and disappeared.

In my mind I pulled them back. I interrupted them. Prodding and patting and shaping, I reassembled them trying to make them friendly to me. I had half a dozen imaginary conversations in which I asked them to come to my slumber party.

"Trixie, I'm having a slumber party Friday night. Want to come?" My voice shook only a little.

In my imagination she straightened up from where she crouched in front of her locker. She slammed it shut. Her Garden Dream perfume wafted around me. She was wearing her chiffon blouse and pale gray straight skirt just as I had seen her only moments earlier. "Oh, it's you."

"Want to come?" I repeated in a faltering voice. I took a step forward in my imagination. The corners of her mouth curved up in a smile. Her glance went past my shoulder. I turned around to see Alice saunter up to us. "You're invited too, Alice. I'm having a slumber party Friday."

"I bet you invited Hilda," Trixie said.

"Yes, I did. My mother told me to."

Alice wrinkled her nose. "Hilda-Dilda."

"She has halitosis."

"She has B.O."

"She's such a dope. Aren't you worried it'll rub off on you, Juliet?"

The blood beat in my ears, my heart pounded a drum.

Alice winked at me. "Wipe your mouth. There's something yellow on your lip."

In my imagination, I scrubbed my mouth with my open hand. Alice and Trixie exchanged glances. I stammered and cleared my throat. Alice elbowed Trixie with a gleeful expression and bumped her with her hip. Trixie burst into a laugh.

I turned to Trixie and cleared my throat again. "I apologize for our fight. I didn't mean what I said about Robert being a dummy."

Alice cleared her throat in mockery, did it again hideously, made it a hiccuping, growling, gasping sound.

I withered inside. Curses and insults thickened in my mouth. "You're an ugly frog. Your face is like a shoe."

"You too."

I looked around desperately. "Your skin is like oatmeal. I want to pee in your face." I meant to say I want to spit in your face. "I hate your voice. You have a dumb voice."

"You too, you too," she said in my imagination.

Hilda came over after dinner Friday night.

I wished I had invited others, that I was not alone with her.

She stood in the hall with her too-short red coat, the fabric at her shoulders and waist straining against the buttons. She held a bouquet of dried weeds pressed to her chest—twigs of milk-weed and thistle pods and other kinds of sticks with names I did not know, all tied in five or six lengths of dumb yellow yarn with a knot at each end. I supposed Hilda's mother made her bring the gift. Mother took the bunch and raised it to her nose as if they were real flowers with a fragrance. "What a nice idea," she said. "Thank you. And the ends are tied in knots. What are those?"

"Sailor's knots. My brother taught me." Her face gleamed as if she had accomplished something wonderful. She put away her coat in the hall closet. She wore the same dress she had worn to school, a blue, red, and green plaid shirtwaist that hung below her knees. I was wearing my second-favorite jeans and an angora sweater.

"You two have a good time," Mother said, leaving to go to the kitchen, past the spinnet piano and dining room table.

"We will," Hilda said in Mother's direction. In a happy voice and smiling broadly, she said, "We're just alike, me and Juliet."

"We are not."

"I meant in some ways."

"That's crap." My eyes must have blazed because she took a step back.

"Do you want to play on the piano?" She tried to mollify me.

"No." I turned and hurried up the stairs to my room. Frankie was sleeping over at Lana's house. On Halloween both of them had gone trick-or-treating dressed as brides, but we eighth-grade girls thought we were too old for those games and disguises.

Hilda clumped up the stairs behind me and we played a game of Clue, but my heart was not in it and she easily won. We listened to my records. She smilingly mouthed the words to "Heartbreak Hotel" and "Hound Dog." She told me her big secret that she thought Don Webber was cute and didn't I agree.

Not exactly. He had acne and his mouth was crooked.

We were silent. She stood up and walked to the corner of the room, where she had left her bag. She surprised me by pulling books out. As she put her books at the foot of Frankie's bed, she asked me was I going to college.

"Of course."

She pleated the fabric of her nightgown between her fingers. "I ain't."

"I'm *not,*" I corrected her.

"I'm not college material," she said wistfully. "I'll probably go to beauty school."

I had never thought of her as caring about her appearance. "You want to be a beautician?"

"I don't mind." She reached over to stroke her book, almost to caress it.

"But do you want that?"

"Or maybe a dental hygienist. Momma says I have good hands, steady hands." She held them out in front of her, as if to count all ten fingers—blocky hands, heavy fingers.

Mine were like my father's. I wished they were like my mother's slender fingers. "I wouldn't like to stare down people's mouths all day long."

She dragged her fingertips across her book. The red cover was pocked and the corners were dented. She looked up and brightened. "I might be a secretary. Momma says I have to learn how to spell." She opened her spelling book. "Will you help me with the spelling test?"

A sharp and buzzing feeling lurched through me.

"Will you help me with my spelling?" she repeated.

"All right."

She placed her childish Mickey Mouse tablet at the foot of Frankie's bed opposite me and lay flat on her stomach.

I supposed it was better than listening to her dumb dreams. "Let's work on apostrophes, since you have trouble with them. It means possessive, belonging to someone."

"I've heard that. Explain it again."

"Like the car of Tom is Tom's car."

"What about the dress of Jane?"

"Right."

She was delighted with herself. "And the food of the dog is i-t-apostrophe-s food?"

"No, no, no. Contractions are not the same thing."

The phone rang and I jumped up. Mother answered it. I went to the top of the stairs, thinking it might be Trixie wanting to apologize for avoiding me, but it was Mother's sister. Father hovered near Mother and touched her shoulder reassuringly. I turned back to my room. Trixie had not called to apologize, to befriend me. I was a good person, why did Trixie shun me? My face felt hot, and inside my chest was a cutting ache as of cloth ripping, fraying, slipping out of the hand.

Hilda sat waiting. I explained the difference between *there, they're,* and *their.* I explained *your* and *you're.* We worked on *indivisible* and *noticeable,* on *potato* and *et cetera.* Hilda labored with her pencil, making large loops, her lips tight with concentration. Her skin seemed rumpled and pitted, loose and thick, unattached. The pencil grated across the paper. I thought I could smell the tangy odor of lead and that it seemed to ignite the air.

Hilda sat on the edge of the bed, her tablet in her lap, dangling her legs contentedly, as if nothing in the world was wrong, as if the world were constructed for her happiness.

"Spell *stupid,*" I said.

She slowly raised her face from the paper: the forehead, the snub nose, the wobbly chin. A flush appeared on her cheeks. There was recognition in her surprised eyes. And then tears.

I wanted to hit her, to kick her. Her weakness did not evoke pity but abandonment.

She wiped at her tears with her knobby knuckles. Her little eyes and face seemed moist, glowing. She made her hand into a fist and jammed it against her mouth.

The room seemed to be spinning and I wanted to center it. "Keep writing."

She dropped her fist. "You can't boss me." She clapped her tablet shut and, hugging her books to her chest, tore down the stairs.

My own chest felt blocked. And then released. I raced after her. "Don't leave, Hilda. I apologize."

She stopped. Her lips were closed and seemed to press together and then relax; her throat worked on something. "I hate you," Hilda said fiercely, her eyes dark and open. She pulled on her coat and bolted out the living room door. "Damn you."

The door felt hot against my palms, but of course it was my

own wild blood.

She left our school at the end of the year when they moved because her father found work across the city in a chicken-processing plant, so she transferred to Central. I heard her brother came back from Vietnam. He limped slightly.

Later, Trixie and I became friends again, sort of.

Hilda did not reveal her mystery to me. Someone looking at us from that distant satellite might have surmised we were huddling together for comfort. Circling around, staying near, moving together, and being warm and safe; that we were offering to each other improvement: gifts, pleasures, salvation. That we held on to each other while worlds careened and collided above us.

Maybe I was myself on the way to improvement, catching at it, holding it, being lifted to a place where there was no struggle, no disguise, no separateness, a place where I could see more, or more clearly.

Nice Girls

The summer of 1967, just before our junior year in high school, Doreen (her real name was Dora Esther Gumbel but she wanted a name with glamour) and I worked as waitresses at Lucky's Diner. Lucky had prospered and retired to Florida, and the present owner, Mr. Lefkowitz, kept the name.

One rainy Monday early in June when I arrived a little before five, a young sailor in dress whites, with eyes light and pure as the rain outside, sat drumming his knuckles on the formica table as he surveyed the room—the booths in the front window, the teapot-shaped clock on the wall, the green glass ashtray with a chipped corner. He looked at his watch, and I wondered where he had to be. When he noticed me peering over the half-door at him he smiled, and long lovely creases appeared on either side of his mouth. He pointed at me, as if this were a peek-a-boo game and he had caught me. I went to the back of the kitchen, where I busied myself wiping the shelves, but I could still see him as he shook his head in amusement and looked at his watch again.

Wearing a beige skirt and a beige sleeveless shell, Doreen hurried in through the back door. I admired the way she color-coordinated everything like Jackie Kennedy. She was later than usual, but Mr. Lefkowitz was too tired or maybe too dispirited to scold her. He glanced at her, sighed, and then went back to running his hand through his thinning hair and staring at the unoccupied tables.

Doreen's face glistened with drizzle. She never carried an umbrella. As she tied on her apron, she told me she had seen a poster from St. Luke's Church propped in Woolworth's window. The parish was raising money by raffling a blue Chevy. "Me and you are lucky," Doreen said. She asked if I wanted to go in with her on a book of tickets. Our favorite color was red, but we could always have the car repainted.

I saw the sailor raise his glass. He and a garish, doughy lady at another table were the only customers. "Hey, Doreen," he said. Doreen's head jerked up and she turned from where she was rummaging in the drawer for her order pad. He waggled the empty tumbler and gave her a comfortable wink. Doreen smiled.

"How come he knows your name?" I said in her ear.

She perked up the polka-dotted bow she wore in her hair, and retied her apron tighter around her waist. "I love guys in uniform." Dimples appeared in her wide cheeks. She had a responsive, vivid face.

"When did you meet him?" I whispered.

She made her eyes mockingly wicked and said, "At least he's not from around here." *Here* was Philadelphia P-A. She swayed over to him with a fresh Coke. Whenever I moved my hips like that, I spilled what I was holding.

Doreen put down his drink, leaned against his table, and giggled. I stood on tiptoe behind the half-door. On the radio, Hank Williams singing "Your Cheatin' Heart" trailed off just before the news and, for an instant, the cushioning patter of rain enclosed us.

The sailor was Nicky Honeycutt, Seaman Second Class, here for a few weeks in the City of Brotherly Love, waiting for orders with the rest of his shipmates. He looked childlike, with his close-cropped hair and dreamy, defenseless expression.

I brought him another Coke because Doreen was in the bathroom combing her hair. "Thank you, Miss," he said. His voice was soft as melting ice cream. "What's your name?"

I gulped at this attention. "Susan."

"Oh, Susannah," he half-sang. "I come from Alabama but no banjo on my knee." He seemed to want a welcome, but I had no words for him. "You have a middle name?" Spoken in a warm Southern drawl, this was an easy, undemanding question.

"Just Susan Krengel." I could not tell him my middle name was Fidelity, after my grandmother.

"A nice name. No need to be shy. Doreen doesn't like her name either. Why is that?"

I thought about how Doreen's mother used to play the piano with her long, quick fingers and do card tricks and make coins disappear. Flick, flick, flick, and the coin was gone. "Maybe 'cause her mother died. It was her mother's name."

He sighed deeply and sadly.

"A car accident five years ago." My explanation kept circling around. "The other driver, he was drunk." As Nicky continued to look at me, I stammered out an explanation about Doreen's dad remarrying after the accident.

From beneath his brows Nicky looked up at me. "I was a child when my mother died."

My heart went out to him! He twirled his Coke glass on the table top, leaving a ring of dampness. I would have wiped it up so his wrist would not get wet, but I did not have my sponge with me. I yearned to confide to him how my own life was not perfect, how I felt ungainly and ugly and detested my big nose.

He stopped twirling his glass and grinned past me. "Here she comes, Doreen the queen."

Doreen swayed toward him. "Want another Coke? Or coffee? We fill yer cup all the way up." She crossed her eyes as she intoned the diner's motto.

He smiled, showing flawless teeth, dazzlingly white, white as our refrigerator at home.

She brushed some crumbs off his table. "Will I see you again?"

His hand covered hers. "Tomorrow."

I stumbled away from his table, their table, and tripped against a chair. I did not think they noticed. I studied the front window, spotted by the rain and city dust, with the name of the diner in black letters outlined in gold. I asked Mr. Lefkowitz if I should clean the window. He told me to wait till the rain stopped to clean the outside but that I could start on the inside.

I had felt lucky to be working at the diner. For nearly three months my regular life was suspended: we were not in school, it was my first real job with adults, my parents said I could keep the money to spend as I pleased. And though I was an avid reader, it was a great adventure to be in life itself and not in a book.

Doreen had been working there after school, and when Babs Contini quit to have a baby, Doreen told me they needed a waitress, so I applied and got the job. Mr. Lefkowitz said his patrons wanted good value for their money and we should be prompt. Doreen said they wanted a laugh and we should be funny. ("Tell them the egg foo young is the best thing on the menu." "But we don't have egg foo young." "Exactly. Ha-ha.")

Doreen and I had been best friends since eighth-grade Home Ec (she called it Home Ick), where we both failed our fudge. She read the horoscope column in the paper and explained we were meant to be friends. She said she was lucky and, when we played bingo in German class to learn the numbers, she won a necklace and earring set like Audrey Hepburn's in *Charade*—pink pearls the size of marbles, which she put on right away.

I told Mr. Lefkowitz it was time for my break. I waved at Doreen, but she was ringing up the check for the doughy lady, and then she went back to sweeping near Nicky's table. The hot rain had stopped and I pulled a stool out from the kitchen and sat in the alley beside the diner and felt sorry for myself.

I wanted to be popular, but my hair was too limp and my nose was too big. At first I was working to save money for plastic surgery on my nose.

"Your nose is fine," my mother had said. "It's your grandmother's side of the family. Lots of character—though I didn't inherit it."

"Potato nose, I hate it."

"On the other hand, look at my nose," Mother said. "Barely enough to hold my glasses up. Dumb little button. Oh, I like your nose. I much prefer your nose."

On my first day of work at the diner, Doreen and I had sweated in the steam from the dishwater. After we finished stacking dishes, with her forearm she wiped away the haze from the mirror by the coatrack, smirked, and stuck out her tongue at me. I had hay fever and a scarlet nose. "I look like Rudolph."

"It's not Christmas." Doreen crossed her eyes.

"Look at my nose," I said dejectedly, "I'm a clown nose, a lightbulb. A fire hydrant. Dogs will come pee on it."

"Only really tall dogs."

"I want to get plastic surgery," I whined. "I want to go to a doctor. I need a doctor."

"Your nose is fine," Doreen said. "I wish I had it instead of this ski-slope." Her index finger slid down her nose.

I stared at her in the mirror. I loved my friend, she deserved all good things. "You know what, Doreen, I like your nose, I truly do. How awful it would be to have Trudy Lanza's dumb little button." I wiped away the fog from the mirror and considered my nose. "You're right. I won't spend my savings on plastic surgery." It would take forever to save enough, anyway.

When I came inside from the alley, Doreen took her break out back and Nicky went with her. I started washing the outside of the front window. Probably Doreen was smoking out back with Nicky. She was the one who showed me how to smoke: inhale, inhale, let out, let out—smoothly, lips pursed as if for a kiss. I did not like it much, and she did not make me do it anymore.

Last winter, a bunch of girls were smoking in the ladies' room at St. Luke's Church, and my hair and pink angora sweater were saturated with the smell. My mother sniffed. I told her it was the other girls who were smoking. Fortunately, that was not a lie. I had not been smoking that time. Mother sighed. "I wish you'd find some nicer girlfriends. Girls that smoke when they're sixteen will do anything. They're not nice girls."

I thought we were nice girls. Except for the smoking.

The rain started again. I would finish cleaning the window tomorrow. When Nicky left, he waved at me and winked at Doreen.

I liked her savvy. For example, she told me that my yellow ruffled blouse muddied my complexion. The year before, when her stepmother forbade her to wear makeup, Doreen used Vaseline on her eyelashes and talcum powder on her nose. She was older, having been kept back in school because she had been deathly ill in third grade.

"Everybody thought I was a goner, but you can survive polio," she said. "I needed baths and therapy, but my family—my real mother—loved me a lot." She blew a smoke ring into the air and caught it between her thumb and forefinger. It drifted slowly upwards, wobbling, stretching, breaking, and finally dissolving.

A few times Doreen came to school with a pinch-bruise on her upper arm. "I deserved it," she said. "I sassed back." She pulled her sleeve down to cover the bruise. "I shouldn't have sassed back." She squared her shoulders, but her mouth trembled.

"Does it hurt?"

"Nah."

"Do you hate her?"

"I always hate her."

"Poor Doreen."

"Hell, my dad loves me. When I'm eighteen, I'm off. I'm gone. Watch my dust."

After work that evening we strolled home, splashing through the puddles, swinging our sandals by the straps. We walked barefoot despite warnings about broken glass and dog turds. The warm water squished between my toes; the smell of damp earth filled the air.

Doreen raised her chin and looked at me out of the corner of her eye. "Nicky's going to college when he gets out of the Navy."

"Big deal."

"He has a red Corvette back in Mobile."

"What good does that do here?"

"He'll take me for a drive if I ever get to Mobile. *When* I get to Mobile."

I blew a bubble with my chewing gum. "You can always ride with me in my dad's station wagon."

"Ha-ha-very-funny." She stopped under a streetlight and lit a cigarette. "He invited me to a movie Friday."

"What will your parents say?"

"Dad will understand. The bitch will be the bitch." She made her voice small and shrill. "George, how will she ever learn discipline if you let her off? We said she would be grounded for two weekends. Two weekends. Blah blah blah blah."

"What're you going to do?"

"He's so cool."

"Do you know how old he is?"

"Would you do me a favor, Susan?" She stopped and tossed the half-smoked cigarette into a puddle.

"I suppose."

"I'll tell the bitch I'm working late. Will you back me up?"

"What about the pay?"

"I'll work the early shift and you can work the late shift."

"I don't know. My parents—"

"Tell them Lefkowitz needs you."

"I don't know. I hate lying."

"But it's true. If I can't work after eight, he needs someone else there. Be a doll, be a friend."

It did not seem like too much to ask of a friend.

The next morning, Doreen and I strolled to work together, and the National Guard drove by in trucks. We cast our eyes down modestly when the bold ones whistled. I pulled my arms in, mortified, but nevertheless the corners of my mouth curved up. This was a new sensation, this power to attract interest from passing soldiers, gallant strangers.

I imagined them: boys who were going to be soldiers! Broad-chested and protective, who laughed in the face of death, contemptuous of torture!

I thought such recklessness was endless, such spirit and brag.

Toward the end of June Mr. Lefkowitz hired a new boy, gawky, with sandy hair and glasses. Chester bused tables, washed dishes, and cleaned up. "Don't spit in the soup," he said when I marched past with a bowl of clam chowder.

I had no intention of spitting in the soup.

I held the slip with an order for fried eggs over-easy, and he said, "The cook won't be able to read your handwriting."

The cook was Mr. Lefkowitz. I was proud of my penmanship. All my teachers in grade school had praised it.

"You'll never become a professional waitress," he said.

"I already am," I informed him. "Being a professional is defined by getting paid wages. Besides, I'm not doing it forever."

"What are you doing forever?" he asked.

"Other things."

"What are you doing on Friday? Would you like to go out?"

"My horse, ma'am," Chester said, opening the door of his 1958 Chevy for me and pretending to sweep a hat off his head.

"What's your horse's name?"

"Old Faithful."

"That's a geyser."

"And my Chevy. My old geezer."

"Ha-ha."

Old Faithful got a flat tire. Chester pulled off the road, we climbed out, he walked over to the rear wheel and examined the tire. I felt useless, but at the same time I liked standing off to the side, cupping my hands in a gracious pose, watching him with his sleeves rolled up to reveal his strong forearms. Did he want me to hold his tie?

"No." There was a small, controlled growl in his voice.

He strode over to the trunk to lift out the spare tire, and I heard him say "Shit" and slam the trunk.

I did not wince; I admired his passion.

He placed an army blanket on the ground and knelt beside the car to jack it up. He unscrewed the lugs and fitted on the new tire.

Finally, he shook the blanket out, folded it neatly, stowed it, settled his glasses on his nose, and we were off again.

We were late for the movie, so we drove to another theater. The movie we saw was about an African safari with an elephant stampede. In a disquieting way, it reminded me of when I was little and, on Saturday mornings, used to watch *Andy's Gang*. One program showed shrieking elephants on the rampage stomping Indian boys as they tried to escape. I did not like the movie.

From the partition, Doreen gazed at Nicky, her arms folded on top of the half-counter. She blew aside a wisp of hair. "Nicky is so cute." He sat in a booth by the door reading the sports section someone had left behind, waiting for Doreen to get off work at nine.

"Chester is cute too," I said, as though he needed defending. He was sweeping near the cash register. I thought of qualities to admire in Chester. He would always be slim, and his hair, when it turned gray, would make him look distinguished.

Nicky glanced at us and smiled. His black eyelashes emphasized his light eyes. Doreen straightened up and, humming "All My Loving," shuffle-waltzed over to me. I was filling ketchup bottles by the corner cupboards. She spoke in a low voice. "The only thing I don't like about Nicky, he never has any money. 'Money, honey,' he says to me. We don't go to movies, don't go to candlelight dinners in restaurants." She picked up a ketchup bottle and sighed. "I guess he's not very good about money." She loosened the cap on the ketchup bottle. "I'll have to be lucky and win luggage and cars and things. An Aries is a perfect match for me."

I could hear Chester's broom grazing the linoleum in long,

smooth strokes. There were no cars honking or driving by. It was another slow evening and Mr. Lefkowitz stood out in front, staring in the direction of the new McDonald's two blocks away.

The news on the half-hour repeated how we helped in the fight for freedom in Vietnam. "I'd like some rock and roll," Doreen announced. She cha-cha-d to the old square radio on the back counter and started twirling the dial, but for a moment it was quiet, there was not even static. We had not turned on the fluorescents yet. The sunset colored the room with a romantic, antique glow.

There was a crash. Out of the corner of my eye, I saw Nicky jump up, frantically slapping ice cubes out of his lap. The newspaper slipped from his table. His Coke glass lay shattered on the floor.

Doreen ran out of the kitchen with a roll of paper towels. I reached under a shelf for a brush and dustpan. Chester stopped sweeping and his eyes met mine. Leaning on the broom, he shook his head in disgust. I prodded him. "C'mon."

"What a jerk," Chester said, under his breath.

Nicky rubbed his elbow and tried to make a joke, pointing at Doreen. "Who did that? Did you do that?" He saw the contempt on Chester's face, and looked at the broken glass, the puddle of Coke, and the wet stain on the front of his pants. "Sorry."

I wanted to console Nicky in his embarrassment, to wipe the table and him, to adjust his collar and pat down his hair.

Chester pushed his sleeves up higher, straightened, and headed for Nicky's booth, dragging his broom.

In the middle of summer, Chester quit working at Lucky's Diner because he got a better job with his uncle's construction company. I now saw him only on weekends. It seemed to me he became tan and glistening and fragrant from the sun.

For my birthday, he took me to the Hong Kong Magic Revue, which was playing at the most elegant theater downtown. It was really an acrobatics show with a single magic act, in which crimson scarves were tied and untied and a petite assistant disappeared and reappeared in a rattan basket. The magician, lifting his knees high, stamped in the basket to demonstrate that the assistant had vanished. In this thick, silky dark anything was possible.

I leaned into Chester. "How do they do that?"

He whispered back, "She's still in there, all curled up."

Of course. I wished I had not asked.

This act was followed by an acrobat who somersaulted through first one burning hoop and then two others. For the show's finale, the troupe's clown bicycled around the stage. A woman in a sequined leotard skipped out and jumped onto his handlebars, another on the back rim, a man on the front, until for its last circuit there was a knot of ten people balanced on the bicycle slowly circling around the stage. Chester and I looked at each other, delighted by the boldness and straightforwardness of the trick.

The performers began to detach themselves. A large man holding two women on his shoulders failed somehow, and the petite magician's assistant from the first act fell heavily. For a second her face was contorted in pain.

Two men lifted her from the floor and whisked her away. I thought her fall was part of the act, but she did not return, and there were nine, not ten, for the final curtain.

I never could distinguish what was dangerous from what only appeared dangerous.

"He wants me to do it," Doreen said. "To prove my love. He says I'm cold, maybe I'm not capable of love. He calls me Do-reen the Snow Queen." She sipped her Coke through a straw and chopped at the ice. Her cheeks were bright.

We were on our break, sitting in a booth in the front window. She squinted because of the hot glare reflecting off the windshields of the cars parked outside.

"I wish I would win the car." She closed her eyes and concentrated fiercely, her lips twitching. "Then I could drive anywhere I wanted." The day before, she had bought another raffle ticket at the church. "He's in love with me, he can't stand it anymore."

"This is like *Anna Karenina*," I said.

"What?"

"In the novel, the heroine, she falls in love with Vronsky. Madly, fatally."

"This is not a book." She rubbed her eyes.

"Your eyeshadow is smeared." I pushed around the salt and pepper containers. They felt greasy.

"He's being sent to Vietnam."

I cleared my throat. Vietnam was in the East, near China and India. The Inscrutable Orient, which was romantic but also dangerous. I wanted to tell her that I, too, loved my Chester. I understand how you feel, I almost said. I chewed on an ice cube, even though this was bad for the enamel on the teeth. The sunlight slanted in golden bars across the pavement. "Don't you think it would be nice to be a virgin on your wedding night?"

She lit a cigarette and forced the smoke out in beautiful plumes from her nostrils. She turned her face toward the outside and looked like a movie star with the light glittering on her cheekbones, shoulders, and long, slender fingers. "Sure, but true love is even more important. That's what Nicky says."

I nodded in agreement. She had a point. True love was the most important thing in the world.

Chester's skin was pale clay and his mouth was tight. "We're moving. My family's moving."

I plucked at the skirt of my turquoise uniform. We sat on crates in back of the diner. Across the alley the barrels full of garbage gave off a rotting, fishy smell.

Chester's father had been promoted to division head at Tech

Chemical's plant in Kentucky. I kept stroking Chester's hand and kissed the hard knuckles. How could I live without him? "Chester, I love you. I'll always love you. Forever." The pregnant cat who lived two doors down in Bloom's Used Books sidled up to us, purring and rubbing against Chester's loafers and my thick-soled white oxfords. Doreen and I looked forward to play-ing with her kittens. She stretched, flopped on the gravel and rolled on her back in the warm sun, then got up and trotted down the alley.

"What's the use?" Chester said. "What's the use?"

"We'll write, we'll never really be separated. We'll be in col-lege together."

But, being a year older, he knew more about it.

The following Saturday we drove to Fairmount Park across the river from downtown, where we had gone to see the Fourth of July fireworks with Doreen and Nicky. We double-dated with them just that once because Chester did not get along with Nicky. On the Fourth, the park had been a noisy, churning mill of people, and the sky over the river exploded in pinwheels, foun-tains, and ribbons of color. Three weeks later we were the only ones there in the starless dark.

East Falls Bridge with its concrete and steel beams arced above us; across it traveled the neat geometry of carlights. The smell of clover and buzz of crickets surrounded us. We stood in the steamy stickiness of summer.

Chester had borrowed the family station wagon because Old Faithful was in the shop. He unfolded his brother's army blanket, knelt down on it, and reached deep into his trouser pocket. Slowly his hand came out, holding a thin packet. I did not rec-ognize immediately that it was a packet of Trojans.

Off in the distance, in the low haze of light from downtown, the trees looked like hills. I blinked, and the trees looked like shadow elephants from where I lay on the ground beside Chester, dear Chester. We tumbled into and around each other through the fiery hoops of love.

Mid-August Doreen missed work one weekend. When she came to the diner on Monday she wore a plain gray dress; she bumped into me and dropped a tray of dishes.

"I'm pregnant," she said, squatting down among the shards to pick up the plates that were not broken.

My stomach jumped. I reached for the large pieces of china, stacking them carefully.

She was one muted color, as if her features were wiped off, leaving only the dimples and eye sockets. "Maybe me and Nicky will get married. I can get out of the house. He loves me more than anything." She spoke without inflection.

I did not know what to say. I followed her into the kitchen and tossed the broken dishes in the trash.

That night in my dreams I saw elephants stomping her and the Indian boys on *Andy's Gang* while Nicky, off to one side, leaned against his red Corvette, gleaming tanks encircling him. He had parachuted in to fix a flat tire for Doreen. Chester and I escaped. We skimmed across the grassy fields and marshes.

On the old black-and-white TV show the Indian boys' tunics were soaked with dark stains. In my dream, the faces got scrambled, eyes and eyestalks were mangled, arms stirred about and positioned where legs should have been, skin folded and frilled.

Actually Nicky was never crushed by a tank, never drowned in the ocean. He survived Vietnam. Years later, I learned that he was killed in Mobile in a car accident (the driver of his car, a woman who was not his wife, had been drinking), but that had nothing to do with my forebodings. Chester and I did write letters and did telephone each other when he went off to college. And then we met other people.

Nicky stopped coming to Lucky's Diner. It turned out he was already married. Already had a baby in Mobile.

He kissed Doreen good-bye ("You're still my queen, Doreen") and promised to send money, which he did, a little.

"The joke's on me," Doreen said. "Ha-ha."

Chester asked his friends, and one, who had an older brother, found out the name of a doctor. We pooled our money (Chester contributed the most, because he worked construction) and paid for Doreen's operation.

I went with Doreen to New York City. The city seemed rainy and jangling to me, a loud gray box, and I felt dwarfed by the tall buildings. We did not even see a Broadway show. We took a taxi straight to the doctor's office.

Doreen's father and stepmother thought we were going to visit my aunt. My parents thought we were visiting Doreen's relatives. They thought we were taking a vacation to spend all the money we had earned that summer.

They were right. We did. We spent it all.

II

An easy life does not teach anything.
– Fortune Cookie

'Tis new to thee.'
– William Shakespeare, *The Tempest*

Is This a Stupid Question?

It happened almost a year ago, but don't let anyone tell you the bad part ends. I had another bout of depression last week. I'm back in school now, and we're studying the same things we were studying before.

I filled out a questionnaire that came with my pre-registration form for next semester. The first question was "Are you currently contented as a student at Fitchville State University?" It was sponsored by the Alumni Association. The choices were "Always," "Sometimes," "I don't know," "Infrequently," "Never." To me it is unclear whether they are asking is the university a satisfying place or am I satisfied? I could, for example, be contented as a person at Fitchville State, as a seamstress or a divorcée, as a twin. I could like myself but not the classes. Or I could like the studies but not myself.

The questions are ambiguous.

And they ought to have eliminated the neutral middle possibility to force a choice if they wanted telling results. I have taken a lot of tests: achievement, placement, IQ, aptitude, psychological. I would be a clever testmaker. I should work for ETS.

A marketing surveyor at the fashion mall asked me, "Which word best describes the shampoo's effect on your hair when you like the way it looks?" *Full of body or thick? Shining clean or with brilliant highlights? Manageable or under lively control?* I want lively control.

She did not ask me which shampoo I liked, or which effect I liked, but which word I liked. Isn't that stupid?

In class Mr. Dork (Not His Real Name) says there are no stupid questions. He says the only stupid questions are the ones you don't ask. Which ones are those? I wonder.

Mr. Dork teaches Interpersonal Communication Skills. We learn Listening, Small Group Dynamics, and Interpersonal Communication Facilitation. We spent a class on handshakes and smiles and eye contact. Many students find it fun and valuable because they learn that what was wrong with their interpersonal relationships was that their body language, their posture, for example, was sending a different message from their words, and their lives are cleared up after this class.

Sounds like acne when he says this, I think. Maybe they just grow out of it. Maybe there's hope for me.

Cooper finally left his record album on the dresser in my room at home while I was at school. Actually it was *my* record album and he returned it to me. I had asked him for it at Thanksgiving.

"You'll get it soon," he told me.

I keep replaying the scene in my mind. "When are you going to give me my Everly Brothers back?" I tap him on the shoulder.

He turns around and is wearing the sweater Mom knitted him for his birthday. It is a blood-red sweater and despite my nearness to him—I am only one chair away—there rises between us a mist, a magic fog that curls up and whitens him, that deadens the sound for an instant. He looks like the inhabitant of a fairy tale. And then the spell is broken.

"Amy, you'll get it soon."

What I want to know is, Did he intend to do it then?

Was his expression accusing? Was he depressed? What did his body language say?

He had a scholarship at Carleton. My other brother is still in high school. I'm at Fitchville State. "Itchville" we call it when we're being disrespectful. Or "F You" if we're childish and outrageous. The president is really into athletics, and in a hundred years, if we try real hard, maybe we'll have a third-rate hockey team. Don't get me wrong. I'm not against hockey. But it should be mediocre, not awful. I suppose it's like everything else.

I compare too much.

Our enlightened parents did not dress us in the same colors nor send us to the same schools and activities. Even the vowels and consonants in our names are dissimilar: Cooper and Amy.

Drugs, they all speculated. But his roommate said he would only smoke grass and only occasionally, at parties.

There was no note.

My brother, my living brother, has been quiet these past ten months. He used to read Stephen King and rent George Romero videos, used to call himself Teddy the Temporarily Undead. He has a gross sense of humor, but he is fifteen. He does not watch horror movies anymore.

He still plays baseball, helps with the dishes, and gets phone calls from girls. Teddy is the cute one. I'm the funny one. Cooper was the smart one. Now he's the dead one.

Mom scans the newspapers for stories of kidnappings and children's diseases. She's afraid for Teddy. I don't know what she's studying for me.

She's going to church now. My father was never a church-goer. My father blames her because she wanted Cooper to attend Carleton. My mother blames herself and my father because he traveled a lot when we were little. Nobody blames me for asking for the record album back.

We are . . . were fraternal twins. Now I'm the only fraternal twin left. I'm half a twin. He was fraternal, that made me sororal, sororital? What are you if you're half of a twin? TW? or IN?

Can Mr. Dork answer that?

Is that a stupid question?

I just wanted my record back.

There is this book called *Famous Twins in History* and Shakespeare's kids are in it. His boy died at the age of eleven. Not of suicide, of course. We don't know how he died. I would not have put him—or them, rather—in that book because, after all, he died as a child. The book wasn't called *Famous People's Unfamous Twins*.

I've got a doctor's excuse and most of my teachers will let me make up the schoolwork I missed. Only Dr. Lucy Karkov, who teaches Composition as well as Shakespeare, is skeptical. She has sharp, unhappy teeth. I would not like to be a piece of gristle in her mouth. My doctor's note is ambiguous. It says there was a recent death in the family and I have had trouble adjusting. If they ask, I tell them it was my grandmother who died. Dr. Kaka examines the note carefully, holding it by its edges far from her with two fingers of each hand. The class of hers that I am in is Advanced Expository Writing (we call it Advanced Suppository Writing). She does not believe my grandmother story. I embellish. "We were very close. She loved me a great deal. I lent her books and record albums."

Dr. Kaka glances down at the note and clucks her disapproval at the note, not at me. She is a marvel of self-control. In her chair she swivels back to her mound of papers. I leave with a smile pressed to my face. She accepted my story even though she did not believe it.

None of the other instructors asks to see the note.

Mr. Dork exudes sympathy and sharing, caring behavior. I would rather have suspicion. Mr. Dork is a Pal to his students. "You have a very unique situation," he says.

I don't think it's unique. I wish it were unique.

I have one more instructor to convince about my story. That class meets tomorrow. Questions of Being 201.

Then I will have finished my list of chores.

# # # #

Cooper was a collector: Everly Brothers' music, stamps, World War One model airplanes to fly away in. He said it was the urge to complete things. For his last trick he did the Disappearing Act. He had a great sense of humor. He gets fifty points for that. He loses fifty points on the "Is Your Family Happy?" quiz. It works out even.

How deeply should I analyze this? Is this comparison and contrast? Do I get extra points for finishing early?

Most people want the right answers. I want the right questions. I'm trying to collect the right questions.

Is this shampoo right for you? How about this record album? This college? This life?

What are the right questions? Is that the right question? Is there a heaven? Is Cooper there? I must write that fifty times. Right that.

From now on I'm going to concentrate on questions. How fast does light travel? What does *Hamlet* mean? What are the seven proofs for the existence of God? What are the four warning signs of suicide? How did Shakespeare's son die? And his daughter, the other twin, what happened to her? Why is a preposition something you should never end your sentence with? What's a nice girl like you doing in a place like this?

Open your test booklets. Answer in five hundred words or less. Please write clearly. You have one hour.

Last Week

The phone rings and startles me: I am sitting shivering and hunched over on the edge of the double bed, without Danny.

It's my old roommate, Laurel, reminding me she's coming over in twenty minutes to give me a ride to class. She's respectful and upbeat. My friends are walking on eggshells around me.

"Hey, Kristina," she says. "Elvis is in my lap right now, purring and nipping at my fingers. He's been a great buddy, but he misses you. I'll bring him by and you can give me a cup of coffee. I need it before I face the little dolts."

What she really means is that this is my first day back after the funeral and she wants to help me.

The whole week before Christmas break, the supervisor taught my freshman comp class. He taught thesis formation and supporting details. My notes and transparencies for this coming week are in a neat pile on the coffee table. What I will teach is the syllogism: it is winter and there are no planes overhead; people would fall up without gravity; therefore, gravity is our friend.

I click on the TV while I'm perking the coffee and sit on the sagging mustard-yellow couch. Elvis has used the arm as a scratching post, and the cotton batting shows through. The navy bathrobe I am wearing, actually Danny's robe, picks up the gray fuzz from the arm. When Danny moved in, he wanted to get rid of the couch, but I thought we could reupholster it.

The sound on my old TV is woozy. On the news is a recap of the events of the past year. In November the Berlin Wall was pulled down. Now in the new year people are still celebrating, hugging each other, and they intend to be happy. When the commercial comes on, it shows two guys fishing in a canoe and later drinking coffee on the shore of a dazzling lake in the mountains. I think it must be a father and son. The older man smiles broadly and wisely and lifts his tin cup as if in salute and says, "It doesn't get any better than this." To me that sounds like a condemnation. This is as good as it gets. Better enjoy.

The mirror on the medicine chest has dead spots. I take my vitamin C, my Valium, and Midol. (Lots of medicating going on here.) My eyes are red. My eyes hurt from crying. I feel guilty when I'm not crying. My watery sorrow seems stony and permanent, but it's only been seven days since he died, and maybe the stones of my sorrow will wear down.

Palliatives, lenitives, restoratives, elixirs, nostrums. I like the old words for medicines. I'm trying to ward off evil spirits. I close the medicine chest and search through my cosmetic bag. I select the blue-gray eyeshadow.

She's young yet, she'll heal—I could see it on the neighbors' faces as they smiled consolingly at the memorial service last week.

Take care, I kept saying to people when they gave me their hands to comfort me. I would put one of their hands between both of mine, cradling it so it could not fall. *Touch as a Healing Power* is the name of some bestselling book.

Neighbors and friends said they were sorry. I was not an official member of the family, so I personally will not receive condolences in the mail, but I helped to address the envelopes of the notes from Danny's family thanking friends for their flowers, prayers, and Mass cards. The family added a sentence or two to the stiff square card on which was printed *Your kind expression of sympathy is gratefully acknowledged and deeply appreciated.* While I was addressing the ivory-colored envelopes, in my mind I said, *Of course you're sorry. We know that.*

Mrs. Lockhart is broken. She sat at the funeral home, plump and sickly beige, her hair shaggy, her red nose sniffing from a cold and from grief, hands in her lap tapping, restlessly tapping.

Danny introduced me to his parents at Thanksgiving. His mother and I were washing dishes together, and she told me she had lost an infant shortly after birth. The girl was born prematurely. They had planned to name her JoyAnne. Danny was born the next year. JoyAnne just did not flourish. Something was seriously wrong with her. It was a blessing she didn't survive, Mrs. Lockhart said. But she did not entirely believe it. Why else was she telling me the story twenty-four years later?

Mr. Lockhart did not say much at the Thanksgiving dinner. His new bifocals were giving him trouble. He had been wearing bifocals before, but these were a new prescription. He had to look down through the half-moon in the lower part of his glasses to focus on newspapers or even his dinner plate on the table. He said, "We all have to get used to changes." He's a philosopher. He has read Aristotle and Thoreau and Boethius. I prefer fiction. After dinner he explained about the Wheel of Fortune turning. To me it seems that Danny fell off.

"It was only when I got older," Mr. Lockhart said, "that I collected photographs—if I could find them—of my grandparents, aunts, uncles." He leaned forward. "I wanted to recover my past."

Danny said, "Kristina wants to recover the sofa."

Mr. Lockhart, used to ignoring Danny's wisecracks, slowly turned to me, adjusting his bifocals. "I wanted to know what I had missed."

So it can get worse. Because I will want to recover the past. Or maybe the sofa, as Danny said.

I have thirteen snapshots and three letters from Danny. We would have been a suave, smooth couple, having gone beyond our redneck roots. We talked about living in Denver or San Francisco instead of the Midwest. We were going to have a stylish, grownup life. Where he was raised the towns had these incantatory names: St. Joseph, St. Anthony, St. Rosa, St. Martin, St. Nicholas, St. Cloud. The last was not really a saint, but named for a residence of one of Napoleon's generals.

I have brushed on too much red—I look feverish.

Last autumn, when his kitten, Elvis, had feline leukemia, Danny dug a hole in the yard about a foot deep with the brown leaves swirling down around him in the wind. He feared Elvis would die in the winter and he would not be able to dig into the frozen ground. But Elvis survived. He is part of that five percent of cats who are carriers but who live.

Elvis lives! Danny threw a party then.

And I know all the feeble bromides about making a pearl around grit. But it does cost the oyster, no matter how pretty the necklace is to humans. Divers take the oysters from the seabed and crack them open. Does the oyster care if the Prince buys the necklace for the Princess? Much better for the oyster not to have the pearl, not to have the irritant. Let Mr. Oyster mambo around in his watery ungrave, singing happy oyster songs.

I fasten the gold chain at the back of my neck. Danny gave me this pendant with the teardrop pearl, his own birthstone, in a mock-romantic apology. He knelt down on my tatty carpet and proffered the black velvet box. "I almost threw away a pearl richer than all my tribe."

"Danny, you can be a real dickhead."

"Charming." He rolled his eyes. "Don't cast your pearls before swine," he said, rising and putting his finger over my mouth.

"You *are* a swine."

He sighed theatrically. "How do you say 'sorry' in swine?"

Does Mr. Oyster bring Miss Oyster a pendant as a present? Does she weep for him when he is fished up to the surface? How gritty does that bit of clam shell insert feel to the oyster? How much does the oyster exude in her weeping?

Will someone crack open my shell?

"I just forgot," he said, finally without mockery. He was always late; now he is forever late.

"You kept me waiting in the rain." This was last summer, but when the plane went down it was winter—is winter—and the ground was frozen, so he could not be buried immediately after the funeral but will wait till spring. He fell out of the sky. What was he doing there anyway, right? No business to be there. His friend the pilot was not even instrument-rated and should not have been flying after dark. I could have gone too; I was invited to visit his cousin in Chicago, but I had a paper to finish.

Before the flight to the funeral, the last time I flew was to England two years ago, in the summer, when I was just beginning to know Danny, so his three letters to me were shielded and funny. He described the seminar he was taking on The Fallen Woman in Literature. He joked that Anna Karenina did not exactly fall but jumped.

The fluorescent light above the medicine chest buzzes and flickers: I look as though I am under green water. There are circles under my eyes no matter how much cover stick I use.

When I first moved here, my apartment was almost burglarized. While I stood at the wash basin, in this very bathroom, the ceiling light on, a man's arm thrust in through the open window. This was on a soft summer evening. The window, placed high and in the corner over the bathtub, did not allow the intruder to see someone was in the bathroom. I was motionless, I could have been a stunned bird in a cat's mouth. I said, "Get out," but not sharp and screaming, more the way if you were frustrated you might talk to a pet. The arm withdrew. Laurel was in the next room, in the kitchen, but I was terrified. There was not anything to steal even, because we were only beginning to move in.

The burglar never came back. They say that the thief sometimes hits the same place again. The following year, the house next door was bulldozed to the ground, no other building replaced it, and I now have a clear view to the corner, to the church of St. Jude, which has a dwindling congregation and, across from it, the doughnut shop, the grease and sugar of which I can smell even though my doors and windows are closed up.

I'm finished with my makeup. I will wash it off. I don't like my face without makeup, I don't like my face with makeup. I do and then I undo. I foolishly imagine I have control. Danny and I argued when I wanted to put off getting engaged until I completed my thesis, and he relented. "You win," he said.

I win.

Through the top of the window, where the curtain is pulled back, high above the doughnut sign that looks like a tire and above the steeple with its shingles like barbs, I see a bird sailing in the blue, unsupported air, a graceful black bird. I can imagine it's Danny's plane or soul, but I know I'm only imagining it—the aerodynamic torso spearing the air, a fleck of two white feathers on its cheek, its noble, contented, superior eye gazing forward.

Once, Danny told me about a priest's lecture on eternity. There is a bird that every thousand years comes to sharpen its beak on a glass mountain, and when that mountain is eroded, that is the first second of eternity—that is how the fairy tales and sermons explained time. In other words, this is just the beginning.

Susan's Week

Sunday

I keep a sanitary pad in my purse wherever I go. When I touch it to reassure myself, I can feel the paper wrapper getting tatty and splitting open.

Tomorrow or very soon I will go to Kmart and buy a pregnancy kit, read the instructions, and do the test. I haven't tried it before because I hoped my period would start, because it's embarrassing, because the weather has been muggy, because I've been busy, because I haven't had the time, because I've been afraid.

Even if I do the test and I'm not pregnant, I won't believe it. I won't believe it unless it gives bad news.

I will go up to Wallace as he's reading some anthropology text about the kinship relations of the Trobrianders and say, "Wallace, I'm pregnant." He'll say, "Shit." I'll tell Nora over a bowl of soup and she'll say, in one of her very rational, schoolmarm pronouncements, "Of course the most important thing is to figure out what you want to do and how to control the situation." I'll tell Jeff, and he'll be solicitous and self-sacrificing. I won't tell Mother.

Wallace will say in a generous and matter-of-fact voice, "I'll pay for the abortion." His fine, kind eyes will be focused on the faraway. I wish I could imagine him saying something beautiful and transforming. We cannot fit each other to our separate dreams.

He represents the effortless perfection of America, or what I think that is: smooth skin, straight bones, regular teeth, the heritage of good nutrition and of the affordability of medical miracles. My own mother, the daughter of two Polish engineers, has broad

67

hands and a mole on her forehead. She told me she was relieved that I favored my small-boned American father.

One time Wallace said he believed in ecstacy but not happiness. I replied that his expectations were due to his privileged upbringing, that people who were not children of corporate lawyers did not expect ecstacy. "You misunderstand me," he said, not even raising his voice. "I meant that happiness does not exist except as an occasional spurt of dopamine." I felt sorry for the poor little rich boy then.

Wallace plays tennis well. That's a game which, when I was growing up in Philadelphia, was a bus ticket and a transfer away. He wears Ralph Lauren eyeglasses, not the discount-store contact lenses that Jeff wears. What is most shameful about me is that I like Jeff's adoration. I should just tell him to leave. Nora said, "Your problem, Susan, is you want it both ways—you'll have to let one go." Easy for Nora, who is radical, not divided. Wallace knows that Jeff carries a torch for me, and he feels sorry for him. Sublime lack of jealousy or self-confidence or trust of me or something. Not, I think, indifference. Not that.

Yesterday Wallace wore the sky-blue shirt I had given him. He stood against the square of my window, with the light and melting humidity behind him. The July heat had softened the six candles on the sill into arcs that bowed toward him. He gleamed as if he came out of the sun-soaked sea, a halo surrounding him, spangling him with dew drops, pearl drops, tear drops. Oh, Wallace, Wallace, Wallace. I want you to be my knight in shining armor, my lover who cancels Time and Space, my prince of men who promises eternity and delivers, who strides through this world untouched and always excellent, but I'm not so attached to the you of wry speculation and Armani socks with holes in them, of surprised eyes and sweaty palms on airplane flights. I doubt that I love you, I don't think I love you, I know I don't love you.

You jump right off that pedestal I constructed—but even that you do gracefully.

Monday

Jeff was making calf eyes at me during the Ethics of Newsreporting seminar, and when he saw I noticed him, he quickly put on a neutral face, and that sweetness cut me, his concern for my comfort. I kept running my fingertips over the initials and lopsided hearts incised on the old oak table while Schultzie droned on about participatory journalism. I could not concentrate on the oral reports, but listened to the whine of the lawn mowers outside and, farther off, the sawing down of a diseased elm. Jeff struggled to open a jammed window; the clover smelled dense and green on the stagnant air.

Right after the seminar, Nora and I walked over to the cafeteria. We had salty chicken soup, which I gulped down. She wanted to talk, to tell me she loves the new TV she bought with the money she got for house-sitting, to tell me she received the packet of information about the Peace Corps, to tell me her father is okay. I wanted to wail at her that my problem is much worse and I don't have sympathy to spare.

Nora's father does not have prostate cancer. She was still wound up, happy and intense. "I don't know which is worse, the waiting or the cancer."

Yeah, I said.

Nora chattered away about her house-sitting job, that she had to do some final housecleaning before her professor returns from Europe next week. "I'll miss working in the garden," she said. "I never realized how much I'd enjoy planting flowers."

Nora mocks my bourgeois triangle. She has no use for Wallace and no affection for Jeff. I told her I was trying to recruit for her Marxist cause. Laughing, she patted my back and said, "Come the revolution, I'll put in a good word for you."

My birthday is next week. I'm worried that my graduate assistantship won't be renewed after this year. I'm embarrassed about having to ask Schultz for an extension to complete my seminar paper. I'm behind on grading the exams for my professor.

And I'm deathly afraid I'm pregnant.

I'm not superstitious, but I thought to myself, I'll wear my expensive white linen shorts, that will make my period happen.

What would I offer to reverse this? Money? An earlobe? A finger? A memory of Wallace? I'm stingy. Even now I'm unwilling to give very much. I want to extricate myself lightly, to get off easy.

The news was on the radio in the lobby as Nora and I left the student center. Local anchor Melissa Hanson reported that there was a trend toward threes in window signs—earrings! earrings! earrings! hats! hats! hats!

"Stupid! Stupid! Stupid!" Nora said, as she stopped to light a cigarette in front of the No Smoking sign. Then she shook her head. "Nothing about community involvement and social issues. I'm disgusted. I'd even rather listen to soft rock." After a singing commercial for home insurance, the news came on with an announcement that the most commonly used dry cleaning fluid causes cancer in mice, a report about the violence in Ethiopia, a story about Dr. Christiaan Barnard's intention to stop performing surgery because of arthritis in both hands.

In a world of torture, death, betrayal, where people disguise their faces, where the valve in my father's heart was defective, and my cousin was born with an unconnected nervous system, I hope and imagine to get off scot-free.

Why do I imagine I'm special, that I'll escape?

Tuesday

Wallace prepared eggs Benedict for breakfast. Neither of us had another bite after I told him I might be pregnant. As I tipped my cup, the coffee grounds slid into the shape of a uterus. With the slightest swirl it disappeared.

Now when we run into each other in the graduate office or the snack shop or the library, I can see the intensity on Wallace's face as if there were stones beneath his stretched skin. I want to calm him in my most maternal fashion, to lie to him, to tell him

I'm not pregnant.

I told Wallace I just needed to put clean sheets on the bed for my period to start. He made a stiff smile. We saw each other a hundred times after classes and he tried not to ask, I could tell.

I feel anxious and edgy. I am a timid person. I worry if there's somebody behind the telephone pole or in the alley when I walk home from the library. I'm afraid of breast cancer—one in nine odds. I worry about other mysterious diseases like "Legionnaire's disease," drought in the West, major food shortages in China. But I don't do anything about any of it. And most of all I'm worried I'm pregnant. And then I don't worry about anything.

The Operation Rescue organization will be picketing clinics in Cleveland next week and here after that. I don't even hate them, but I'm afraid of a scene. Nora despises them, calls them birth Nazis. I just don't want to be embarrassed.

Wednesday

I should call my mother because I haven't called her in two weeks, but I cannot bear to hear her loving, tyrannical voice asking me what I want for my birthday. She will be falsely jolly. She will insist that I'm not eating enough, will interrogate and praise me for my few good grades, ask about the Incompletes on my transcript, hector me about deadlines, will not say how much she still misses Dad.

When I was alone in the Office Trailer, Jeff sidled in clutching a bouquet of daisies wrapped in a cone of newspaper limp from the humidity. "An early birthday present," he said. The air conditioner burbled noisily and I was feeling sorry for myself, listlessly leafing through the papers and exams on my desk. It had been exactly a year since we met in Griffin's seminar on Mass Media and Social Institutions, when Jeff transferred into the class late. He extended the bouquet toward me. "I'm not asking you for a date," he said. "I'm happy to see you, that's all."

I had tears in my eyes, and he started singing in his thin tenor,

"Oh, Susannah, now don't you cry for me . . . The sun so hot I froze to death, the weather it was fine." I laughed and said that was wrong, he'd gotten it wrong.

His devotion makes it worse. He's not even asking me out anymore. He stares at me and smiles. Last month he said he wouldn't ask me to marry him if I would just let him be around me. We can't control our desires. If I could, I would love Jeff for his sappy admiration.

Outside the trailer, a train roared by and rattled the tin roof. We didn't have anything to talk about, so we talked about the three kittens in his garage. One is a white male and deaf. What a bad mother she was to abandon them, I joke lamely. Jeff doesn't know what to do because the landlady does not allow pets. He's hand-feeding them and sitting perfectly still on the cement floor as they come to sniff him. They romp around him, chasing leaves, pouncing on his toes, mewing at him in their treble tones, demanding and dispensing affection.

Thursday

I bought a pregnancy detection kit. This one had two tests in it. Do I expect to get pregnant again? Why did I do that? It's called First Response ("Easy," "1-step," "three minutes"), as if it were baby's first words, or a missile launch. There were four or five different kinds at Walgreen's, in monochrome narrow boxes with serious words on them and no pictures of fluffy-haired happy blonds.

The checkout clerk, a lady with bifocals, was arthritically loading a white plastic bag with the candy bars, balloons, card, and birthday candles of the grandmother in front of me.

"I can take care of someone here," the high school kid said behind me from the counter where you leave film to be developed. I was wondering if I should pretend I hadn't heard. I could see out of the corner of my eye that he'd leaned forward. He'd say it again, I knew, only louder.

I turned away from the grandmother and her shopping cart

full of presents for children.

The teenage clerk's skinny neck and short hair and big ears made him look even younger. As soon as I handed him the package, he hurriedly dropped it into a bag and didn't meet my eyes. I felt sorry for embarrassing him.

At home I read the instructions a hundred times. The detector was a rectangular plastic rod the thickness of a few popsicle sticks, with a pair of windows smaller than fingernails cut into it. I was supposed to pee on this, hold it in the urine stream five seconds, hold it vertically and not splash on the windows. My heart hammered as I tried to manage all this.

I blinked and two lines appeared in the windows. It wasn't even the stipulated three minutes.

Shit. I was pregnant.

Friday

I told Wallace about the test. He took a breath. His eyes scooted away. And finally he asked what did I want to do. (I know what I *want,* but not what to *do.* I want time to run backwards, that's what I want. I want the sun to stand still, the wind to be soft, people to be kind, me to be kind.)

I will call my doctor, make an appointment. I'm glad it's the weekend and I don't have to do anything. I'm heavy, lethargic, as if I were deeply pregnant. It's my mind playing tricks. I feel nauseated, hot, woozy. A sharp, cutting pain in my stomach rises and arcs acutely; my stomach is having sympathy pains with my uterus.

I endlessly analyze the future: I could get married; I could have the baby; I could give it up for adoption; I could *not* have the baby; I could drop out of school; I could marry Wallace; I could marry Jeff. . . . That's as far as my imagination stretches. No—be imaginative. I could go to the moon; I could buy leopard-print tights and become a rock star. I have an infinite world of choices. I could kill myself.

Not funny, Susan.

This is not the year to become a mother.

I'm a modern woman. I don't have a pinpoint of guilt about it. What is this malaise? That I am making a decision for forever? That I will never have a son or daughter? That this decision will be like every other: little by little, forever. But it's not true. I can always have a baby later.

Wallace and I have talked about marriage obliquely, but we don't really love each other. We are both clear on this, which is miraculous: (1) that we should be certain (when we're uncertain about advisers, about dissertations and prelims, about where to live and so many other things) and (2) that we should both agree.

Friday evening

As I was getting ready for bed, I had a cramp that started in my abdomen but shot out to the root of my scalp and to the walls of the room, which spun around me.

The dizziness passed, I put on my nightgown, I finished getting ready for bed. There was a warm, stringy blood clot, for a moment, in the shape of a thorn in the toilet. I knew what it was. My womb expelled the zygote. Another spasm. This wretched tissue, my exhausting, humiliating interior self has finally been extruded and expelled. But I don't feel celebratory.

I'm very tired.

Saturday

Nora is sleeping in my bedroom, and I'm sleeping on the couch. While she was staying at her adviser's house, on the night before he came home from Switzerland, a burglar broke into Nora's empty apartment and took her Sears TV, her stereo, even her cheap Japanese guitar. When I drove over to pick her up, her skin felt clammy and she looked flat, the way a frightened animal will collapse, hoping the predator will have mercy this time. She's afraid to go back to her apartment. "Just superstition," she said. "And normal terror."

Sunday

In the middle of the night, I woke up with the heavy thought on my tongue—I will die in twenty years. I don't believe it, of course, but I'm drawn to analyze it. My subconscious is perhaps guilty about the spontaneous abortion because I wished it; or my life feels chaotic and I'm depressed; or I'm ill and tomorrow is my birthday and I don't want to telephone my mother or wait for her call. The rational part of me is not superstitious and does not believe in this message from the dark, the knotted sleepy self. This is not guilt, just normal terror.

III

You will be asked to adjust to a new environment.
– Fortune Cookie

The litel spot of erth, that with the sea
Embraced is . . .
This wrecched world . . .
– Geoffrey Chaucer, *Troilus and Criseyde*

Woman in Peril

As she had done every evening that summer, for half an hour or so before she went back to work on her thesis, Sarah sat on a wobbly lawn chair in the garage, trying to be absolutely still. The cat treats on the garage floor lay in a line leading toward her sandaled feet. She thought she could hear the vague rumble of the train, coming across the river from Manhattan. She was not sure whether the sound was reassuring or ominous, but of course it was just the subway, grinding by.

Neither Sarah, whose apartment was upstairs, nor the three undergrads who rented the first floor of the brownstone in Brooklyn Heights owned a car, so the garage was used for storing cardboard boxes. Late in May a mother cat had weaned her three kittens and left them to fend for themselves. Now the kittens, only partly tame, crept to within a yard of Sarah and stopped at that perimeter, sitting on their haunches, studying her.

One evening at the beginning of July, they approached slowly, slowly to her toes, their unblinking, wary eyes fixed on her face or hands. By then Sarah and Raymond were sleeping together, and she told the kittens about his wife. She sounded falsely chipper, even to herself. The garage smelled musty because it had rained that morning. The rafters looked dark and damp.

Sarah stretched out her hand. "Silly me. I'm twenty-six. I know better. This is not how I was raised."

Cleopatra answered with a small, strangled bleat.

"You're probably right, but that man is the light of my life, my Holy Grail, my moon." She shook her head. "Boy, am I in trouble. Here's one for you, Cleopatra." Sarah tossed a cat treat to the calico kitten. Cleopatra rose on her hind legs in a leaping twist and batted it down to the ground with her front paw. "You *are* the Willie Mays of cats. One in a million. This relationship, on the other hand, has no potential. I should get out of it right now."

In the loft, the orange tiger, lolling on his side with his round head hanging coyly over the edge, yawned. "Thanks for listening. Got to read Malory." She reached to pet Cleopatra, but the kitten scooted away. "Have a nice day."

Sarah had met Raymond Nilsen because he was the editor assigned to her professor, Donna Cage, who was writing a book on the child-in-peril theme in popular literature. It was an orphaned book after the original editor had quit, and Raymond was drafted from his usual post as a very young, very junior editor of romances and horror over on the trade-book side. One chapter included films, and Raymond tried to persuade Professor Cage to devote more of the book to movies so that it might sell better. They were meeting in somebody else's office because Raymond's was being painted, and he was not able to find the sales figures to prove his point, but he continued, "We've all seen these films. Child kidnapped, mother upset, dog frantic." Sarah watched Raymond watching her out of the corner of his eye for her reaction to his joke. Pleased at his attention, she laughed brightly. Her gauzy rayon skirt felt heavy and crooked. She tugged at it to make it drape evenly across her knees.

Professor Cage rushed off to another appointment but Sarah stayed behind for some papers, and Raymond asked her if she would like a tour of the publishing house. "Yes." She was eager. For her graduate assistantship last year she taught at-risk students in the remedial writing center, so editing seemed glamorous. Raymond introduced her to coworkers, most of them as young as he was, and she peered into cubicles cluttered with manuscripts and books. She knew editing may have been as unromantic as correcting comma splices, but it felt exciting to be part of the enterprise of literature.

He stopped in front of his own small office and joked self-mockingly that his window faced an alley but that alley led to 53rd Street and 53rd Street led to Broadway. He had long eyelashes and his eyes at the outer corners drooped slightly to meet his smile. The new paint smell stung her in the forehead. She tiptoed on the spattered dropcloth and looked out the window to the brick wall of the adjacent building and down the seventeen stories to where a trash can from a restaurant was rolling and spilling into the alley. She thought she could see a white dog rooting around in the garbage. She took a deep breath as if she were plunging into a pool of cold water and pivoted toward Raymond.

He had taken off his cement-gray jacket. She noticed he was missing a button at his cuff. It crossed her mind that if he were to wear that shirt to her place, she would sew on the button for him. He talked nervously about the history of the publisher and the current rumors that the firm might be swallowed by a corporation which had started out in the manufacture of toilet paper and sank to printing tabloids. She acknowledged his anxious joking. She wished it were in her power to keep his job secure.

Out in the hall, next to the huge potted palms beside the bank of elevators, he appeared frail and tangled. She allowed herself to think he was an endangered creature. He mentioned he was in the middle of a divorce—"An amicable separation. Meg said the Big Apple was full of worms and went back to Wisconsin." The elevator chimed and they rode it down.

Sarah had told Raymond she needed to prepare for an interview for a part-time job at a community college, and he walked her to the subway station. They lingered at the subway entrance, but finally she made herself say she ought to go. Raymond took the escalator down with her and waited outside the turnstile until she walked down the stairs and onto the hissing, pulsing train.

The next evening Raymond showed up at the screen door of her apartment on the second floor. She unhooked the door. He stepped out from the granular shadow of the neighboring building and into her kitchenette. He held a bottle in a bag.

"To celebrate," he said. "You seem sad." He looked like a tall, thin monk wearing wire rim glasses and a Hawaiian shirt.

She forced a wide smile. "I didn't get the job."

"I picked up some cheap champagne." He busied himself with removing the bottle from the brown bag. "You'll get the next job."

"I thought I'd get this one. Silly me."

She could see him dip his head forward slightly, starting to do something difficult. "Here's a toast"—he boldly raised the bottle, but his eyes were tentative—"to failure."

She grasped the cold bottle. "To failure." She led him to the other end of the apartment and the platform couch strewn with pillows. The heels of her sandals clattered on the linoleum; she slipped out of them. On the wall was a print of Bosch's *Garden of Earthly Delights*. In the left panel of the triptych Adam and Eve were being introduced to each other. Their faces were smooth and innocent as eggs, before mortality and distinction pressed them and their descendants in the central panel, where naked people clustered together instinctively, most of them with faces still calm and vacant under the glassy turquoise sky, which in the right panel, erupted into night and clash.

She saw Raymond staring at the print and said, "Shel preferred abstract art." Raymond glanced at her and pointedly did not ask who Shel was, so she did not ask if Meg was pretty, if Meg was a good cook, if Meg was funny. Sarah told Raymond that her cat chose the print because in lower Eden there was a spotted cat carrying some unlucky rodent out of the painting. A flash of amusement in his eyes, he tipped his head to one side and said her cat had good taste. She brought wine glasses while Raymond worked the cork with his thumbs until it popped and the white vapor smoked from the bottle. The most interesting feature of her apartment was a window of glass blocks in the far wall, the kitchen wall. In the winter it showed milky light; now in midsummer at sunset, hot yellow washed over everything. "Welcome to my hovel."

Uncomfortably he admired her needlepoint pillows and her. "With the light in back of your hair, you look like a Botticelli angel."

She pretended to preen, lifting her nose higher. "My hair *does* cover my jug ears."

"I really mean it."

The fruity champagne fizzed on her tongue. "I know it." They sat on the couch. She sipped more champagne and kept observing him and his sweetness, his nervousness. She wanted to find a flaw in his fine face and temperament. "How could you leave your wife?" She had been thinking about this during the day, all day.

"*She* left *me*," he snapped. He closed his eyes and scrubbed his face with one hand.

"Maybe you should have tried harder."

"If she takes her Zoloft, she'll be all right."

"She's in pain."

"Yes, well." Raymond stared at the floor. "It wasn't like a book I could edit. There wasn't anything I could do anymore." He raised his eyes to Sarah. She thought he was asking for understanding and compassion. "At first it was okay, and then Meg didn't like being married. I said it would be the same if she were married to anyone. Meg said I was trying too hard, hanging on. I said I had strong fingers. She said she was the one with strong fingers, she played piano, she chopped bok choy, she didn't need me." He shook his head stiffly. "It was a struggle. Even the good times."

"Good times are always a struggle. Look at us." She moved closer to him on the couch. She straightened his peacock-blue collar so that the palm fronds on either side matched. Already she was behaving in a proprietary way.

After they finished the champagne, she peered into the refrigerator. There were three eggs in the egg carton. She squinted at the expiration date and sighed. The bread, however, was not green yet.

She set out a jar of peanut butter and a pot of coffee on the vinyl tablecloth. It had a cheerful design of colored bubbles like a child's balloons rising in illusion out of the flat white surface.

He teased her. "I didn't know you were domestic."

She pursed her lips and waited to be amused by his next line. "Mmmm."

"The worst kind of saturated fat is in coffee." He leaned forward, his voice somber, scary, the voice of a character in a horror movie. "And the most dangerous carcinogen is a mold that grows on peanuts."

She made her voice small and wounded. "But I love peanut butter and coffee."

He chewed into the sandwich ravenously and spoke with his mouth full. "You are such a good cook."

"I know it. I'm writing a cookbook." Now she leaned toward him, opening her eyes wide, imparting a shocking secret. *"The Love Canal Cookbook: 101 Easy Toxic Waste Recipes."*

"Cookbooks always sell." He swallowed the last bite. "I win," he said. "I made you laugh."

Two weeks later she was fixing pork chops for Raymond in her tiny, sweaty kitchen and telling him that her parents were proud of her working on a doctorate. Her dad had asked, "How'd my baby get to be so smart?" Sarah was not sure she had gotten to be all that smart.

She told Raymond about her sister, who fell in love with a cabdriver she met and married one week later.

Raymond told Sarah that even as a teenager he wanted to edit great books.

She told him about her cat, Peanut, who was a formidable hunter in spite of the bell on her collar.

He told her that he and Meg had separated once before, but he persuaded Meg to come back and try marriage counseling. "A mistake."

She told him about Shel, the man she had broken up with last winter. "Would the self-help books call my relationships an addiction or a pattern?" She meant the remark to sound sprightly.

Raymond straightened up, turned off the water, and put the lettuce on the drainboard. "I wouldn't like to think of myself as a squiggle mark in a pattern."

"Sorry," she said and, coming up behind him, caressed his forearms and lightly kissed the back of his shoulders. "Sorry. Sorry."

He pressed against her. "Don't stop," he murmured. "Feels good."

"Am I forgiven?"

"Maybe in a while," he said. "I like this."

The oven timer dinged. She nuzzled him once more. "Besides, you're nothing like Shel. You're not older, and you don't play chess. Shel never let me cook." She bent over the oven to check the orange-sauced pork chops and scalloped potatoes on the bottom shelf. The heat from the mouth of the oven fanned out and encircled her.

She let the cauliflower head fall into a pot of boiling water and turned to open a can of cheese soup for the sauce. She paused. The smell was steamy and ripe. She could taste the cauliflower and pork chops on the air. Her stomach seemed to crumple up, but the wave passed. "Maybe my menu wasn't such a great idea. Everything is sort of yellow. And it's hot with the oven on." She pulled her blouse away from where it stuck to her collarbone.

He finished slicing the mushrooms and, toweling his hands, said simply, with no sarcasm or mockery, "Anything you fix is fine with me."

"You sound like my darling mother on Mother's Day." She felt happy and uncomplex and full. To ask for more would be greedy.

Peanut meowed outside the screen door. Raymond unlatched the door and Peanut trotted up to him to sniff his trousers. She wreathed in and out between his legs while he stood as if he were afraid to move, as if there were glass shards all around him.

Sarah scooped Peanut up in her arms, scratched behind her

ears, and felt her purr in her fingertips. "She likes you." Sarah buried her chin in Peanut's fur. "Peanut was hit by a car and her pelvis was broken in four places, but she completely recovered. A couple of months ago she carried a baby robin all the way up the stairs. I tried to get it away from her, but she snapped its neck." Raymond winced and Sarah shrugged. "Hey, that's the way it is." Peanut's purr grew louder and she thrust her tiny chin out to be scratched. "Peanut would hate it if I took in the garage kittens." Peanut's breath came out in a contented whirr. "They already sit next to me if I don't make a sound. There's nobody else to take care of them." Peanut struggled to be let down and sauntered away.

The sound of an accordion drifted through the open kitchen window. In the apartment below, someone had put tango music on the CD player. Sarah's bare feet sensed the vibrations, a pleasant thumping insistence. Raymond stood silent, and she asked, "Are you okay?"

"You make me jittery," Raymond said. He gulped a mouthful of air. "Off balance."

"Sorry, I don't mean to." The pan of potatoes she held was hot even through her oven mitt. She herself felt jangled. Outside her window, the streetlamps came on in cones of harsh orange; children's voices shouted that it was time to go home, that Mom was mad, that it was getting dark. Her wrist trembled; the potatoes were burned around the edges; her ears were ringing.

"I like it," he mumbled hoarsely.

She placed the pan on the table. She felt a fine rash of perspiration on her brow and upper lip. She wiped it away with her forearm. She glanced at him and thought he almost swayed; she flicked her eyes toward the pan and the trivet and the table. "My mother would say the light shines through you. She would say you should put some flesh on your bones."

He set plates on the table. "Sounds like my mother too."

She moved the chairs closer together. "My mom likes to cook and she's very Catholic."

"But you're not?" In the deepening dusk the pupils of his eyes were large.

"When I was little, we were churchgoers. Big time." She remembered the beeswax candles flickering in the dark, the spicy incense wafting from the censer, and on holy days the thin hymns that floated upward, filled the church, and threaded inside her. "Now I've become a skeptic." She shook her head wistfully. "Last winter Shel and I drove up to the Catskills, and on one turn the wheels hit a patch of ice, spun out, and skidded off the road, flew. I knew the car was out of control. Knew it. And I couldn't do anything about it. *We're going to crash* was all that went through my mind. Not my past life, not regrets, not the future I didn't have, not an act of contrition, not heaven. And there was just the shortest instant that I liked it." A fork fell out of Raymond's hand. He bent down to pick it up. "The car wound up in the ditch." She meant to push the pan toward him with a pot holder but it slipped, and accidentally she touched the rim with her bare hand. She knew she burned her hand before she actually felt it, before she could pull back. She began blowing on where the welt would rise.

He circled her wrist with his thumb and forefinger, and lifted her hand, palm up, to his lips. His mouth was warm. The brilliance of the window with the orange streetlamps behind his head dazzled her. She wanted to turn away at the same time she wanted to fall into it. Swooningly she thought he could be her all-in-all. She could be his. She closed her eyes until the whole world became static-blank.

The dream job happened in October when a teacher left mid-semester, and it was only a fifteen-minute ride on the F train.

And yet.

She and Raymond walked along Fulton Street under separate umbrellas in the cold drizzle. Meg had telephoned from Eau Claire to tell Raymond she was coming back to New York. Raymond stepped off the curb when three teenagers, not holding umbrellas, not wearing raincoats, shrieking among themselves, shoved between them. Raymond stepped up on the sidewalk again. A car horn blared and Sarah jerked her head. Meg was not doing well, he said; she was depressed and guilty. An old couple, both with brown mufflers wound around their necks, strode grimly arm in arm toward them and bumped Sarah's shoulder.

"I'm writing a thesis," Sarah said. "I haven't learned a thing. I'm like Lancelot with his stupid holy devotion. I haven't learned a thing. They should revoke my degree. Take back my high school diploma even." She felt as if the icy wind were raking at the skin on her face. "You won't leave me, Raymond, will you?" In avoiding a puddle, she brushed against the hem of his trench coat. "Out in the cold, un-Rayed, de-Rayed. Derailed and dismayed?"

He stopped under the awning of a jewelry store and closed his umbrella. "My little petunia, I crush you to my powerful chest," he said, French-rolling his *r*'s and narrowing his eyes.

"You're making a joke."

"I don't know what else to do." Slumping against the damp wall, he seemed out of jokes.

The rain ticked on the awning. His face, reflected in the depths of the window, was like a blank outline of a country she could not see inside. Beyond his face, under the shop-window fluorescents, glittered diamonds, emeralds, and opals. Her own rings, agates and rhinestones, did not glitter the same way under the seventy-five-watt bulbs at home. The proprietor brought down the grate on the window and began to remove the jewelry from the display case, taking out the necklaces from the back, then the pendants and rings.

It was dark by the time they walked back to her apartment, and the rain had ended. The street lamps made the night sky a rock-cloud above them. As they entered the garage he stumbled on a brick that had been left by the neighbor children. She caught his hand so he did not fall. She pulled the chain on the lightbulb, which glared and swung over the space that was all edges and shadows. He stood barely inside the entrance of the garage while she poured cat food into the bowl. The reddish nuggets clinked against the side. The kittens watched Raymond from their loft but would not come down even when he clucked to them. Mr. Rochester paced, stopped, and sat back away from the edge of the loft, staring. He dipped his head, as if asking to be petted but afraid of it.

"They're almost tame," she said in the habit of recitation, "I bet I could bring them indoors." She needed to fill their water basin. "Cleopatra's trick is to play catch. Mr. Rochester's trick is to hide."

"What's Lancelot's trick?"

"Lancelot's trick is to be a sweetheart." She wanted to burrow into Raymond, shelter herself in him, be in his pocket, in his head, in his breath. "Like you."

He gave a hard cough, his eyes startled. She could hear a neighbor's car whine next door, but the engine would not turn over.

She filled the water bowl from the outside faucet, and they climbed the stairs. Her ankles felt heavy, her knees stiff; this must be what it was like to be old and unwell. She held on to the handrail. The wet city gave off a soaked-clay, matted smell. The key stuck in the lock, but she jiggled it. The apartment had a rainy, closed-in odor that was smothering. She could not see Peanut anywhere. Turning, she called for Peanut. Panic washed over her. She could not remember if she had let Peanut out. Her heart thumped as she walked toward the closet. Meowing, Peanut ambled out from under the bookcase, yawned, stretched her front paws forward, and then flopped on the rug.

They took off their coats and shoes and clothes. Her naked skin felt chilled and sticky.

Above her bed there were stripes on the ceiling from where the curtains did not quite overlap to shut out the light from the streetlamp.

Raymond twirled and patted her hair against the pillow. "I don't dislike cats. I just never had any. I don't understand cats, their appeal."

"They're all different."

"Is something on your mind?"

"You know what's on my mind."

He brushed the hair away from her forehead. "I'd give anything to not hurt you. Anything."

"Would you give up Meg?"

He held her in his arms again and said nothing.

Finally she pulled away.

Peanut sidled next to the bed and Sarah snatched her up. "Peanut would like me to give up the garage kittens, but I don't know how to do it." Sarah held her with both hands. She held on tight. "I'm going to become one of those crazy ladies who feed the stray cats in the neighborhood. Who trudge all over the neighborhood leaving food in likely places." Peanut wriggled away and jumped off the bed.

He whispered. "You're a good human being." He kissed her fingertips. "An angel."

"Not good enough," she said. "Apparently."

He lay back on the pillow. He closed his eyes. "We promised not to talk about that."

"I'm breaking my word. I'm no angel. Me and Mae West." She took the top of the blanket in her hand and began folding it into pleats. Outside, the wind had risen to a low hiss. When he did not say anything, she started talking again. "Peanut's my first real cat. Before that, Fluffy belonged to my sister and Midnight to my brother. She's my lucky cat."

"You all right?" he asked. Sitting up, he massaged his brow as if his head ached.

She swung her legs off the bed and tripped over his loafers. She wrapped her old chenille bathrobe around herself. "What are you working on?" she said, louder than she needed to. She stood by the window, but did not look out. She shivered and retied her belt, cinching it tight.

"Not a child-in-peril this time but a woman."

"A woman-in-peril novel?"

"Actually, a woman in Cleveland."

"Ha," she said, "ha."

"This maniac stalks her."

"Is he in love with her?"

Raymond's mouth turned down as if he had bitten into something spoiled. "Sarah, he's a maniac."

Now she felt foolish because he did not understand her joke. *She* did not understand her joke. Maybe it was not much of a joke. She stepped from the window toward the futon with the Bosch print above it. "Love makes the world go round. Or is it flat?" She tried to revive the lame joke. "But what if he did love her? What if he got de-maniacked and became a devoted lover? What if he loved her more than anything?"

"They'd be in a world of trouble."

"And what if she loved him back? What if she gave him everything, and they lived happily ever after? What if she gave him nutritious peanut butter sandwiches? De-molded. And coffee with no saturated fat in it—using only a pat of margarine for flavoring."

"Silly her," he said in a subdued voice. Her futon seemed vast as he reached across it for her hand. "Silly them."

The next day he knocked at the kitchen door and let himself in. She sat on the couch with her lap full of needlepoint work. She heard the grinding and wheezing of trucks outside and felt a draft until he shut the door.

He took off his tweed jacket and placed it over the back of a kitchen chair. He folded his scarf in equal lengths and tucked it into the sleeve. He was not usually so meticulous. He stood with his hands in his pockets, jingling coins. The thin October light washed over his paleness and tiredness. He put on what seemed to her a polite, strained smile as if he were addressing the mayor of the city. "You look domestic," he said, attempting their old joke.

She said sharply, "You too." She pulled a thread through the canvas backing and snapped it with her teeth. "This is what we do when our lovers go on the Crusades. I'll start with this pillow, but I'm going to do a whole tapestry, a whole wall—roomfuls— a whole house, a whole city."

"What is it?"

She held up the square, which was the size of a coffee-table book. "My own design. Venus and Cupid. Now only the face of Cupid is done. How many pins can fit in the head of an angel?" She let it drop into her basket of yarn.

"Very good," he said. "We need to talk."

"It depends how long my lover will be away. I mean whether it's a pillow or a wall hanging." Peanut jumped into her lap and nuzzled her knuckles. Sarah massaged her lightly between her ears and to the side of her jaw. "How long will my lover be away?"

"Sarah."

Peanut jumped off her lap. "You're going back to Meg."

"She called me last night, and I went over to see her."

The air shifted in the room. There was a sticky clot at the back of her throat that she could not swallow. She ran to the sink for a glass of water and gulped half of it down. "Boy, was I wrong. I pictured myself as the lady of the castle. All along I was the heathen girl he met on the Crusade. The one with the flashing eyes and the sultry smile. Just R-and-R in the desert." Raymond tried to hug her but she shook him off.

He dipped his head uncomfortably. "I always liked you. I still do."

"I always loved you. I still do."

"Sarah, I can't leave her. She's not managing well."

"It's not fair." Even to herself Sarah sounded feeble. She felt translucent, like paper-thin eggshells, like watery tea. "I always admired your honesty."

"The last thing I wanted to do was hurt you."

She thought he tried to hold his chin steady.

"Meg wants to give the marriage another chance. I'm not

sure." He faltered. "And you're so strong, independent."

"I'm strong and you're honest. What could be better. No problems here." The top of her head was shooting toward the ceiling. "I'm going to take in the kittens," she said. "Peanut's just going to have to put up with them."

"I don't know if I can do this anymore," he said, his voice breaking.

"Me neither."

But the next evening he brought another bottle of champagne, this time an expensive Moët, and sat down at the kitchen table. Her parents had called to invite both of them for Thanksgiving Day and, ashamed of her evasiveness, she had put them off with some excuse about how Raymond might be gone for a convention.

The late sun seeping through the glass blocks rippled like cold water. She lit the scented candle in the middle of the table. The sandalwood fragrance spiraled around them. She waved out the match languidly as if counting time to a calm hymn. In the distance, she heard the anguished wail of a siren, but here the light was easy and protective.

His fingers traced the red and yellow circles on the shining white oilcloth. "I'm reading a manuscript in which this spirited young widow with flashing eyes and gleaming raven tresses loses her adorable baby in a shopping mall. A child-in-peril story again."

She could see bluish shadows under his eyes. He wore a dark, ill-fitting sweater. She wanted to smooth it into shape. "Will it sell, do you think?"

"She leaves the baby in a shopping cart while she rushes in to buy some—"

"Let me guess—peanut butter." She opened the cupboard to get wine glasses.

"It's a first novel." His voice wobbled. "They don't believe in the project if they give it to me."

She held the wine glasses tightly by their stems. She leaned a hip against the sink and put on a joking rumble. "Do I detect self-pity in my man of men?" She glanced at him sideways, afraid for him and his pain.

He tilted his head to one side, slapped the table, and peered around in a mock-challenging way. "Men? Where are these other men?"

She set down the glasses and turned to him across the kitchen. His neck was slender in the large sweater somebody else had knitted for him. He blew a wisp of hair out of his eyes. The refrigerator hummed. The floor tipped and she slid toward him on hot ice. "You're all my men, all my world of men," she whispered.

He smiled, but not happily. "Then you're in a world of trouble, my dear."

She saw in his eyes bleak affection for her and hard pity for both of them. "I know it." Peanut trotted in and wound in and out between her ankles. Sarah stooped to pick her up and caressed her. Her fur was warm and smelled of sunshine. Sarah's eyes flicked away from Raymond. She said, "I know it."

Listening to Stravinsky

Last month they cut down three full-grown elms on our street. It took an hour and a half and, with ordinary brooms, they swept the twigs toward the tall, boxlike orange truck with its funneled chute angled into a huge engine that sucked in every last leaf and stick and mulched them. A half hour per tree. On the door of the truck was lettered the name of the manufacturer, Whisper Chipper.

When I first heard the high, menacing buzz, I was washing dishes. It sounded like a chain saw, like a drill to my skull; I could feel its grinding, pulsing hum in my teeth. Our cat, Paris, his ears flat back, dashed into the kitchen, and I hurried out to reason with the person attacking our porch. An absurd act, if I really believed someone was so close and that I was going to go and find out about the mistake or ward them off with a soapy dish sponge. And then it turned out to be the city workers cutting down diseased elms.

I watched them hack the branches, feed them into the chute, where they were torn into chips and—*zow zoop*—no more disease and beetles, no more tree. Those seven men swept the street briskly and meticulously, just as if their mothers were coming to visit. They probably have to be thorough because of the beetles.

I was relieved: that was one situation I didn't have to do anything about.

Even shopping malls are not safe, but they don't want you to know that. Your child can be stolen right from under your eyes. At one of the malls, Southdale or Rosedale, I think, a two-year-old blond girl disappeared. The police were notified and sealed the mall at the doors. They found the little girl in the washroom. This woman had taken her. She had scissors in her hand. She was cutting the child's hair. She had already dressed her in boy's clothes. All is not well.

Things are not going well between us, between Perry and me. I don't know when that started. Was it when I went back to college? Or before that, when Lila was born?

Maybe I should visit my sister in Chicago. She'll know what to do. Sitting there in her immaculate house, sipping a mineral water, she will say she never liked Perry and she never understood what I saw in him all these years. She'll tell me to get a divorce and good riddance. She's probably right.

But I don't think she'd care for Val either.

Perry is a librarian. People think that librarians are harmless and cerebral. Actually, he's natty and clever and maybe murderous. He wears silk bowties and has his hair styled by a New York City–trained barber. And in our early days he used to make me laugh. Last month, over and over, he played his new record of bagpipe music. He glared at me when I walked into the room, his fingers twitching. "It's Scottish war music," he said.

I didn't even know I wanted a divorce until I met Val a year ago. He was my instructor at the university. His name is really Valentine, but everyone calls him Val. Me too. Only in my rapturous daydreams is he Valentine of the strong thews, Valentine of the blue eyes, Valentine of the gentle visage, of the silver hair. He is open and light and large. Perry is small and dark and closed. It is ironic that Perry should be the one who is honest. "We need to examine the circumstances and see what we can salvage," Perry said when I told him.

Here is how I met Val. I am twenty-seven and he is forty-two. I was working on my bachelor's degree, as much to get away from my babies as to have the degree. I was majoring in English, which Perry thought was impractical if I wanted to have a career. What I wanted was to be a different person three hours a day, an adult, a nonmother. I love my babies, but they are not everything.

Val—Dr. O'Neill—was teaching the Milton class. I do not like Milton because he is so unloving, so finally certain about the world and human behavior, and such a blind bully that he makes me intolerant of him.

I said this to Val after class last year. He smiled indulgently at me, thinking no doubt of the self-assurance and pomposity of callow youth and invited me for coffee at the student center, but I had to pick up Nancy and Lila at daycare. After the next class, I invited him for coffee, but he had an appointment with his dean, whom he characterized with atypical hyperbole as having a diseased and knavish itch for power. Even though, as a student, I paid no special attention to academic bureacracy and gossip, I wanted to be interested in what interested him. I listened and nodded knowingly. I was determined to prove to him that I was no ordinary student; not that I was extraordinary, just that I was not mediocre. Already I was trying to please him.

I am a timid person, so I am surprised that I asked him that second time and more surprised that I asked him yet again. I was flattered that someone listened to me, heard me, even if I thought he was overly kind in attending to a woman who was merely a dilettante, a drifter, an escapee from housework.

There were three of us; another woman, Clara Hopkins, stayed after class and decided to join us for coffee. She *loved* Milton, she said, her voice loud and smug.

I kept quiet.

Val didn't say anything.

She thought Milton was an inspiration to us all. Her brown hair fell in greasy strands about her round face. She was twenty or so and had bumpy skin and a dark down on her upper lip. Perhaps she wasn't quite so grotesque. Perhaps I resented her being there with Val, being a superfluous tenant in my world. And what can a person do about bumpy skin anyway? She continued to spoon banana cream pie into her little circle of a mouth. "I love the notion of *felix culpa*. That a mistake, a sin, could be better than purity."

"More precisely," Val said, "it has to do with the joy that comes through the redemptive act that atones for the sin."

My cup clinked on the saucer. "I disagree with both of you. I don't think that joy can make up for pain. You grab what you can before the ride is up." That was pretty daring for me. I was being the riotous hedonist, the insatiate sybarite. Why did I wish to appear an advocate of debauchery, when even in our sex Perry and I pursued nothing more adventurous than the missionary position? Foolish, foolish woman. Perhaps I was trying to outrage Clara. She did knit her brow and glare at me.

Val cleared his throat (for effect?—which sounds more theatrical than he is) and cast a measuring glance at me and broke into a smile. "I would not have taken you to be such a voluptuary. Go for the gusto, hmmm?"

"Mock on, mock on, Voltaire," I said.

Val's wife has multiple sclerosis. Nobody knows what causes it; it is a "mysterious disease," which makes it sound romantic. There are theories about infection by a virus, or a deficiency of particular minerals or enzymes, or an allergic reaction. Nobody knows for sure. The sheaths of the nerve cells are destroyed and scarred. The hardened scar tissue cannot, of course, function as nervous tissue. Her body in the very act of repair was betraying her. She can just barely walk with the aid of a walker, which she thumps down ahead of her and leans on as she pulls forward her heavy, almost useless legs. The disease may soon claim her sight and speech too. She is losing more and more control over her body even as, unknowingly, she controls more and more of our lives.

There are periods of remission, followed by periods of progressively worsening symptoms, of greater paralysis. Val won't leave her. They have no children. I suppose she is, in a way, his child to care for. I happened to be watching from across the street when he wheeled her out of the grocery store, her lap and legs covered with a brown plaid blanket. My rival—such a shriveled token of flesh.

Later, I asked him why he didn't go shopping by himself after getting a list from her. He shook his head at my obtuse question and explained that occasionally she wanted to go to the store as she used to do. She has had multiple sclerosis for ten years, and will have it for ten or twenty or thirty more yet.

So is that what I'm doing? Just waiting for his wife to die? What does that make me? A ghoul? One of those people who stop to stare at accidents or roadkills? I don't like to think of myself that way, but I have to admit that if I could cause her to die in a wish, I'd do it. That makes me a murderer in my heart. I would not wish her pain, but I would wish her out of our lives. He won't divorce her while she's dying. He won't marry me. It occurs to me that we three (and maybe four if I count Perry) are married by chains of love and disease.

My dilemma: Perry wants me to live with him, but I'm certain he doesn't love me. Val, who does love me (probably), doesn't want me to move in with him.

I hate my life, what I've become. Maybe I am a terrible person, what the nuns called a "reprobate." Perry would think so.

I wrote out a check for a hundred dollars to the Ethiopian Famine Relief. And then I didn't want to hear about it anymore, didn't want to see pictures of sticklike humans walking on dusty paths, of babies with insects buzzing around their mouths and eyes.

Perry's friend, George, used to try to cheer me up when I had one of my mopey moods. He said I was lucky. He's in a wheelchair. He caught polio when he was eleven. It's true that I've never suffered from polio or fought in a war or endured famine, but I'm not "lucky." Every one of those things may happen to me yet. Already my marriage is foundering. Terrible things may lie ahead. I might be picked off by a sniper. I could be maimed in a car accident, made so ugly that even darling Val wouldn't want me.

I cannot imagine a life without my lover, although I'm living it now, and obviously, I lived without him before I met him. Like the song, "I ache for him, it's fever love, only monkey in the blood." I do believe love makes people crazy, its immensity and danger and despair. I'm not being whimsical. There are all sorts of craziness, and love is one kind. I think someday the scientists will discover this for a fact. They will find a chemical in the blood that makes a sane person insane, that gives a person maniac desires. Last March, when I hadn't seen Val for thirteen days because the winter quarter was over, I waited for him in the rain outside the student center housing the campus theater, so it would seem I bumped into him by chance. For half an hour, like a fool, pacing back and forth, dripping, my fingers red and cold, I was hoping to catch a glimpse of him.

My friend Winnie had been taking his spring class and said he recommended the Bergman movie on campus. I arrived late for the film after an evening class. For the fourth time, I was studying the poster with coming attractions on it. I had turned away from the door and was startled by his voice in back of me.

"Can I give you a lift home? Juliet?"

"Oh, hello. Dr. O'Neill."

"Were you just in the theater? I didn't notice you."

"I've seen *Cries and Whispers* before."

"What did you think of it? Did you like the movie?"

"Sort of." I decided to be brazen. "All those quivering psyches and throbbing questions. . . ." I shrugged.

"You're a tough one," he said with an amused, skeptical expression, as if he didn't wholly believe his comment. "Let me give you a ride home. You look cold. Where do you live? In town?"

"Thanks, I've got my own car, thanks." I wish I'd walked, so I could accept his offer.

"I see." He pulled on one glove.

I didn't quite know what to do. "This drizzle is awful."

"Yes, it is." He pulled on the other glove.

"I hope it doesn't continue. It wasn't raining when I went to class." I could feel my bangs damp on my forehead. "I think it's letting up a little."

"A little, yes," he said, politely examining the sky.

"For the past half hour it's been just a slight sprinkle."

"You've been out in the rain for a half hour? Out here?"

"I left my umbrella at home." I hadn't thought to bring it. Questions passed across his face, but he didn't ask them. I sneezed.

"I feel responsible," he said, with more humor than remorse.

"I didn't catch the cold from you," I said rather sharply. A student's crush might have been droll to him, but not to the student. "You're absolved."

"My umbrella is big enough for two. I should walk you to your car."

"To ease your conscience?" I did not want to be a moral obligation.

"Something like that." He put up the umbrella and extended his bent arm for me.

I walked close beside him under the canopy of the umbrella with the soft rain promising spring. The puddles beneath our feet reflected the lights around us and shimmered into iridescent ripples moved by the invisible wind.

We stopped next to my Datsun. "This your car?" he asked. I nodded. "Would you like to have a beer in the Rathskeller? Or do you have to get home?" His voice faltered. "You probably have assignments to do for class."

"I'd like a beer," I said.

We saw each other often after that.

This was last March. I was not some sex-starved adolescent, newly charged with hormones. I was a twenty-seven-year-old married woman with two children and a husband.

I'm coming to hate Perry, but I never feel hate for Val even though he won't let me move in with him. Perry calls me crazy, says I will eventually come to my senses, says I'm lucky to have someone who'll forgive my sluttish behavior.

My neighbors tell me I should "go into" real estate, that I like people and would do well. They don't really know me if they say that. I only *appear* to like people. Inside I'm willful, greedy, inconsiderate, flighty, selfish, moody, and lecherous. When we were living together, Perry said all those things about me except the last. That one he saved for when he found out about Val.

That spring Perry got weirder and weirder. One time in May he stayed up past midnight playing bagpipe music on the stereo and making chocolate chip cookies. He brought a plate with two dozen of them stacked on it into my bedroom, the guest bedroom actually. I was sleeping there because I had the flu and could not bear to be touched. I was sneezing and coughing. Perry wanted me to eat the cookies. "I don't want any. I ache all over."

"I baked these for you."

"*You* eat them."

"I'm on a diet."

Perry is one hundred forty pounds and five-eight. I sighed. "Have you checked on the girls?"

"They're sound asleep. You ought to have some cookies."

"Sure, Perry. Leave them here."

"You need your strength. You're ill."

"I just want to rest."

"I'll go open a can of chicken soup."

"Don't you listen, Perry? Doesn't anything get through that goddamn skull of yours? Are you crazy or what?" Without a word, he stalked out of the room, and I could hear him in the kitchen, washing dishes and clanking pans. In a childish fit, I spitefully whacked the rim of the plate, which was on the edge of the nightstand. It fell and spilled the cookies on the shag rug.

Perry came in, ridiculously holding a tablespoon in his right hand as if he'd just finished stirring the pot. "Now look at what you've done."

"Stop shrieking. You'll wake the children."

"Shrieking? Am I shrieking?" He waved the spoon at me. "You're the one who should lower your voice."

Lila started to whimper in the next room. It wasn't a pained cry, just a fretful whine. "You've wakened her," I said, some malicious gladness in my voice.

"Why did you throw the plate down?"

"I didn't. The dish was on the corner of the stand." I sat up and swung my legs onto the floor. Lila was still crying fitfully.

"You did," and his eyes were fierce and unsparing. It's difficult for me to remember exactly what happened next and in what order, but I think (and I must not sanctify my own behavior, for surely I contributed to the heat of the events) he tossed that stupid spoon at my bare feet on the floor. And then (I don't think it was before, although perhaps it was), I kicked the melmac plate toward the baseboard, and at the same time, I gave Perry a shove. I told him I'd been seeing another man. He called me a lecherous slut. I wanted us to separate.

He caught my wrist, squeezed it, twisted it. We are not violent people, but we came close to it that time. He released my wrist and whispered, "You're crazy." He turned and left the room.

I said he was becoming weirder, but perhaps I'm the one. He says I'm crazy.

He's not a brute. He probably has all sorts of wonderful qualities. And when I married him I'm sure I loved him, although it's difficult for me to remember now. And I'm certain I'm coloring this, since it's one side of the story only, not a balanced report.

Maybe he's going crazy. I don't know. He says I'm the one. Maybe he's right. Maybe we're both right.

Can that happen to two people who know each other so well they both are infected by the same lunacy, a contagion we're both susceptible to by virtue of years of proximity?

There have been many episodes of mass hysteria. Surely twin hysteria is easier to buy. He says we're not getting a divorce, he won't permit it.

⁑ ⁑ ⁑ ⁑

The other day I came home and found my Datsun with its right fender smashed in. Perry said he had borrowed the car and that he accidentally ran into a parking meter. I would have believed him except for what happened after that.

The following week he borrowed my car because his was at the mechanic's. I was climbing the stairs to the second floor when I heard tires squealing. I stopped on the landing. A current bored through to my bone marrow. Afraid of what I was going to see, I peered through the window curtain. Perry had pulled out of the driveway into the street and was turning the car in a semicircle, aiming its right fender at the stop sign across the street. He deliberately rammed into it. The sound of metal against metal was surprisingly soft and fleshy. I did not see the signpost move. Suddenly it was at a drunken, tilted angle. Fear filled my mouth, hot and dry, cleaving to my palate and arching back to my throat.

That was what he wanted to do to me. I would be one of those people who are killed by an insane family member. I used to wonder how it was possible that the family didn't notice that the person was insane. They know. There just isn't anything to be done. They must wait for the death stroke.

That afternoon I moved in with my friend Winnie, who has an apartment across town. I did not tell Perry. I took my babies and two suitcases and our cat. Winnie thinks I should file for divorce. She has a small room with an extra couch. The girls and I sleep in there. I brought a sleeping bag. I'm not so fearful anymore.

Val judges me, I see it in his face. He does not altogether approve of me. Behind those eyes, he thinks I'm an adulteress.

He denies it.

How can he? I *am* an adulteress.

"I would do anything for you," I said. "I would climb mountains. I would move mountains. I would . . . do anything."

"No one's asking you to do anything." The lower part of his face stiffened; the long creases on either side of his mouth that were dimples in his youth (I've seen photographs of him as a beautiful child) deepened.

He must've thought I was reproaching him for not divorcing his wife. Perhaps my extravagant protestations *were* a means of accusation. But he did not come back with reciprocal protestations.

I so wanted his approval. Fickle, fallible woman. As if I could clothe myself in his smiles or eat his good opinion. I shunted wisdom aside, clasped dark impossibility to me. I pretended I was in paradise. Would I behave thus when I was fifty? Would I flirt and entice, preen and simper and paint my face? I marvel that I was so prodigal, that I did not care what I spent, what I lost.

I thought Val was reckless, but he wasn't. He was shot through with decorum, morality, duty. He'd been raised Catholic. I told him I was baptized a Catholic but confirmed a heathen. He didn't think that was funny. He had his lectures to prepare. Next week classes would start.

I had to share him not only with his wife but with his students as well. Never be the other woman, I said to Baby Lila on my knee.

Just once I wanted Val to be swept off his feet, rash, irresponsible, foolish, wild. He supposed double adultery was wild enough. He had to drive his wife to the clinic in Rochester. "I'm tired," he said.

We didn't even make love before he left town.

In the morning, I took the kids to the baby-sitter. I was nervous, jumpy, perhaps because Val was away. I decided to walk to the grocery store, which is a half mile from Winnie's apartment. I bought a light shopping bag of groceries. "Love" was printed in a flourish of red letters on the brown bag.

Two blocks from the store, a large van had stopped at the corner. It was medium gray, with a high cab, snub nose, and rounded ends; there were windows in the side panels, but the glass was of the type that would not let you see inside. It was a smooth gray beast with black window eyes. It waited at the stop sign an inordinately long time, and my anxiety returned. I finally crossed not in front of it but parallel to it, and it moved past me slowly, the engine whining. I took a deep breath and, when the van was gone, concentrated on the arching elm trees, their high leaves trembling in the slight breeze. I shuddered. As I crossed the next street, to my right I saw the gray van outlined against the rosy morning sky. This time it sped down the road toward me as if to run me down. It screeched to a halt at the stop sign and proceeded past me.

The driver could have been lost, someone new in town who got turned around or who was looking for a particular address. Or it could've been Perry.

I walked quickly. There was nobody else on the street. My breath came rapidly. I crossed the third street from Winnie's apartment and saw the van to my left. It drove by as I reached the curb. Its horn blared.

Now my breath was like a jagged knife. I tried to quiet my rising panic. Perhaps the driver was making a square around this neighborhood to familiarize himself with the area. I could always run up to someone's door and tell them the van was following me. But it wasn't exactly following. It was making a circuit around me.

As I watched the van drive away, a teenage girl walked past me. I took incongruous comfort in that. I was not alone. I caught up to her, then passed her, listening for her footsteps in back of me. Nothing could happen if she was in back and saw everything.

The click of her footsteps diminished. I slowly swiveled around to see her blond head disappearing around a lilac bush that bordered an unpaved alley. And behind me, gaining on me, was the large gray van, sunlight glinting off its sleek, impervious surface.

But it didn't follow me. It rolled into the alley.

I walked the next block so fast I almost tripped. I was making myself hysterical, I said. If I believed the van was evil, I should've rushed into the alley to help the girl. If I thought it was harmless, then why was I nearly running?

From the right, the gray van rumbled through the intersection in front of me.

I did run the last block to Winnie's house. I hurried up the back steps, glancing behind to see if the van was still following. My hand shaking, I fitted the key into the lock and let myself in. I put down the groceries and walked on tiptoe into the living room to look through the front window. No traffic, no cars at all. I went to the front door for a different angle on the street. Coming toward the house was the gray van. But it hadn't seen which house I entered. It didn't know. I watched it through the window in the door. It couldn't see me, could it? I stepped back as it drove past. But there was a window to my left. Was I silhouetted against the light?

The next day I checked the newspaper. My breath was ragged, as if I'd been running. No violent assaults were reported. No special brutalities.

I wondered if it was Perry. I wondered if he'd figured out I'm with Winnie.

That evening as I was playing records Val had lent me, I was startled by the chime of the doorbell. Perry, vaguely threatening, vaguely penitent. He stood in the doorway, would not come in. He wants me and the kids to move back. I told him I'd think about it, although I have no such intention. The van was parked across the street under an elm tree. He said he rented the van because his car was being repaired.

Winnie tells me to get a lawyer. I'm going to do it. I'm going to do it tomorrow.

Val and I meet when his wife is at the hospital. He brings records over. The other day we were listening to *The Rite of Spring*. Val was explaining to me about harmony and dissonance, about resolution and shifting rhythmic patterns. His wife is pretty sick now, and Val and I get to see each other often. Because his neighbors might suspect, he comes to Winnie's apartment. Her neighbors don't care.

So we make love. That is something. A person shouldn't wish for everything. People should be happy with what they've got.

Frankie's Story

The waitress brings Frankie's second margarita and sets it on a small scalloped cocktail napkin. In the corner is the name of the restaurant, The Happy Hombre, and above that a line drawing of a smiling man wearing a sombrero. Frankie starts tearing the edge of the napkin into fringe, neatly, in parallel rows, beginning with the side opposite the smiling face. "We're getting a divorce," she says. "That's the first thing we've both agreed on in a year."

Juliet swallows as if something sticks in her throat.

"Cheer up. It's okay." Frankie's smile is rigid as she stares at the napkin, and for a second she seems to be enclosed in a grayish film like balloon rubber or a plastic bag that might stop her breathing. "It'll be okay. That's what Ted and I want. This is not a tragedy. Life goes on, they say."

"Have you told Mom?"

"That I haven't done." Frankie turns the corner of the napkin and starts tearing the other edge. "Mom will say, 'Well, Frances, at least you don't have children.' And she'll mean, 'Well, Frances, you've disappointed me again.'" Frankie raises her glass and twirls it by the stem. "No little baby-sized souvenirs of Ted. I'll tell her just before I leave."

"So it wasn't that Ted was working in Chicago. I wondered why Ted didn't come with you."

"Ted *is* busy in Chicago." Frankie puts both hands around the bowl of the glass as if it were a crystal ball and stares into it. "Ted has someone else to come with."

"What?"

"Sorry," Frankie says. "My mind's in the gutter with him and his slut. She's a nurse where he's doing his residency. She's not even pretty. And she has a four-year-old kid. Can you imagine Ted with a kid? He wouldn't have one with me."

Juliet reaches toward her sister's hand at the same moment that Frankie raises it to cover her eyes. The shadow of the ceiling fan flashes across Frankie's face. Juliet thinks she can feel the whirr of its motor and hunches her shoulders in the chill.

Frankie looks up again. "I've been depending on Barry, Sympathetic Neighbor." She stretches her fingers out. The pink nail polish is chipped. "I'm trying to prove I'm still attractive, but it's a bad time to try." Frankie lifts her drink in a toast. "No foreign entanglements, that should be my policy." She drinks from the glass. "Marriage is hell. Divorce is hell. I shouted that at Ted. You know what he said? 'Frankie, my dear, I don't give a damn.' Great sense of humor he has, my husband, my soon-to-be ex-husband." She reaches for her purse and places it in her lap.

"This Barry, what's he like?"

"Like Ted. I need someone else to put through school, right? I must look like a scholarship program. He wants to study law. He's seven years younger." She tosses a pack of Benson & Hedges on the table and searches in her purse again. "That's the fashionable thing, a younger man."

"Do you love him?"

Frankie finds the lighter in her purse. "Ted bought me this lighter for our first anniversary. What am I doing with this? I quit smoking and look at me. Poison, I love it. Nicotine, nitrosamines, cholesterol. Bring it on. Feed me with a forklift." Frankie taps a cigarette out of the pack and lights it. "Barry wants to marry me. When I was twenty-four I thought the sun rose and set on Ted." She sighs. "God, I hate myself for smoking." Frankie stares at the lighted cigarette, then brings it to her lips. "Ted told me he's in love, that I should try to understand, that he has never felt this way before." Frankie forces the smoke out through her nostrils.

It plumes out and powders away into the dark air. "I could have killed him then."

Juliet reaches across the table, but Frankie pulls her hand back. When they were kids, Frankie's cat was hit by a car. Frankie stroked it, prayed over it as it wheezed, but Sweetheart died at the vet's office. Frankie would not let anyone comfort her then, either.

"You wanted to take care of me—my wonderful big sister," Frankie says. "You held my hand in the backseat when Mom drove me to the dentist." She looks away. "I've monopolized the conversation."

"This is not a timed debate." Juliet pauses. "The way I remember it is that you kept both your hands on your mouth, but I'll hold your hand now."

"No need. I'm perfectly fine. I've got a great dentist—though my personal doctor is not so good. How are you?"

"I'm looking for a new job."

"I mean with Val."

"We don't want to get married, we don't want to split up."

"Why quarrel with perfection?"

"We're a habit."

"A good habit," Frankie says quickly.

Juliet hears the insistence and yearning in Frankie's voice and nods. She lifts her eyes to the door as it opens. The place is not busy, maybe because the weather is sunny and people are avoiding the indoors, maybe because the road in front is dug up.

Three plump middle-aged women, giggling and squirming, seat themselves in a booth across the room from Juliet and Frankie. They ask the waitress to light the candle in the squat red glass on the table and, for a flickering red instant, they look like the three Fates, except they are jolly. One of them takes a cupcake out of a square white box and sets a candle on it so the waitress can light that too. She says something with great animation.

The young waitress laughs at the joke. "Are youse ladies visiting from Paris or Rome now?" she asks in her Pittsburgh accent.

One of the ladies has large, glittery glasses with out-of-fashion bows that swoop down and then up to her ears. She waves at the waitress's corny flattery, and they all laugh. Juliet would have guessed they drank wine coolers, and she is surprised that they order merlot.

"I don't want to talk about Ted anymore." Frankie says this in a resolute way, but her posture looks soft. She straightens her shoulders. "How's your teaching?"

"Ninth graders—they're so twitchy."

"Hormones forever." Frankie inhales deeply. "If you're serious about quitting, come to Chicago to look for a job. But I'm just babbling. Of course, you can't. Val has tenure at the university. I was just thinking you could stay with me for a while. If you wanted."

"The last time we lived together we were ready to disown each other." Juliet tries to make the comment jokey.

"How is that possible, two charming women with all the graces? Beauty, intelligence, tact."

"I don't know. We're all too smart for our own good. We keep inventing things. Love, for example."

"Do you mean that?" Frankie's irises are blue skies. "Mom and Dad were married all those years. You really don't believe in love?"

Juliet sees the answer her sister wants. "Of course I believe in love. And then he died. They must have loved each other." She says it louder. "Of course they loved each other."

There is a hoot of laughter in the booth across from them, where one of the ladies brushes cake crumbs from her polka-dotted bosom.

Frankie tilts her head. "Will that be us in twenty years?"

Juliet looks across at the women and wonders that herself.

The front door opens and a woman comes in out of the hot sunshine, but it's not the friend Juliet and Frankie are waiting for. She stands by the front counter. She wears a pink tank top and a skirt that floats in the cool dimness. The door has shut, but she still seems outlined by light. The waitress has chosen rollicking music on the jukebox.

A tall man strides from the back of the restaurant to the woman in pink. She turns to face him and laughs in surprise and pleasure. He carries her pink cardigan over his arm. He drapes it over her shoulders. She takes his hand as it rests on her shoulder, raises it to her lips, and kisses his fingertips.

Frankie lines up two rows of taco chips on the table. "I've been in the marriage wars and I want to surrender, but they're taking no prisoners." She sweeps the chips into the basket. "There's something wrong with me, isn't there? I'm defective somehow. I'm too ambitious or too greedy or I'm not persistent enough or I think too much—or do I ask too many questions?" She shakes her head. "Or maybe there's only so much love, commitment, whatever. And it gets passed around, doled out. You have to wait in line and not go to the bathroom or you'll miss your share." She rubs at the table next to the ashtray as if there were a spot. "I say to myself, 'No whining, Frankie, no whining.' Maybe I'll win the Publishers' Clearing House Sweepstakes. Only yesterday I mailed my entry and told myself, 'You may already be a whiner.'" Frankie grinds out her cigarette. She glances at her watch. "Lana did say she was meeting us?"

"She might be late because she's visiting her uncle." Juliet keeps her eye on the door. Plants in clay pots hang from the ceiling, the kind that don't need the sun. Or maybe they are replaced when they droop. Juliet asks, "How's your job?"

"When I get back to Chicago I have to start planning the spring seed and seedling catalogue. From asters to zinnias. Then on to vegetables. Tomatoes—Italian plum tomatoes, Jubilee tomatoes, Beefsteak tomatoes. Then more gigantic tomatoes, tomatoes Tyrannosaurus. The tomato that devours Cleveland. We ought to name one for Ted's new *friend*. A bleached blond tomato—a Big Boob tomato." Frankie's voice is loud enough that the three ladies turn to look at her. She stops and takes a breath and lowers her voice. "You know, they were called love apples in France. And people here thought they were poisonous."

Juliet sees Lana enter the restaurant and waves to her. Lana wears a sundress and a broad-brimmed hat and walks toward their booth with small, quick steps on high, tottery heels. Lana lives outside Boston and is married to a computer programmer. They have three children.

"Great to see you guys! Juliet, you look terrific." Lana sits down beside Frankie and hugs her. "Frankie, you've cut your hair!"

"Can't be a hippie forever," Frankie says. "Time to calm down, fatten up, buckle my seat belt."

The waitress comes over. Frankie does not even look at the waitress, whose dark lipstick and mascara make her baby face seem even younger. Frankie orders a third margarita although she hasn't finished the one in front of her.

Lana admires the waitress's dangling earrings and asks for a scotch on ice. The earrings are open hearts on wires that jingle when she moves her head. "Where's Ted? I expected to see him here." Lana grew up across the street from Juliet and Frankie, and they make it a point to keep in touch. They see each other once a year, during the summer usually, when they come back to visit their relatives in Pittsburgh.

"Ted and I have separated," Frankie says. "We've portioned out the furniture and now we're divvying up our friends." She fixes her eyes on Lana. "I get you, I saw you first."

Lana's face is serious. "Of course, I'm your friend."

"Ted is in love with another woman," Frankie says. "They're going to get married."

"Oh, honey," Lana says in a small voice.

"No, really, I'm all right," Frankie says. "It's just my pride. Or is it that I'm drunk?" She puts her hand up. "Don't say anything. I've been filling this place with sad stories." Frankie raises her eyes to the walls and ceiling. "Enough is enough. Say you're my friend."

"Of course. Yes, we're friends. Always."

"Till death do us part?" Frankie says.

Lana nods slowly, acknowledging Frankie's irony. "We're the three musketeers. Remember our club?"

Juliet says, "The three Bs." Neither Frankie's nor Lana's last name has begun with a B since they married.

Frankie inclines her head toward the women across from them. "Is that us in twenty years? I'm probably the one with the red weepy eyes."

"I think she's happy it's her birthday," Juliet says.

Lana leans over the table to look at them. "They're kind of cute. I hope I'm the rich one, the one with the diamond as big as a goose egg." The ladies notice Lana is staring at them, but she is not embarrassed. She waves at them.

"Listen to me, I sound like a granny." Frankie lights a cigarette and looks at the lighter in her hand. She holds it out to Lana. "Did I ever show you the lighter Ted gave me? The inscription is from *Othello:* 'And when I love thee not, Chaos is come again.' In college I helped him with his paper on *Othello,* so he made a poster for me with that line. He could've been a calligrapher, he has wonderful hands. For our anniversary he had the jeweler engrave it on this lighter. We met in an honors seminar. 'Literature of Love' it was called. One day we read 'Frankie and Johnny.' Just the words, without the music. After class Ted came up to me and made some witless joke about was I like the song, did I keep a gun in my kimono. He was such a romantic." She sighs. "He still is."

"I think maybe you are too, Frankie," Lana says. "A little."

"Nope," Frankie says. "I'm hard. That was the worst thing he said to me. He said I was hard." She turns to Juliet. "Do you think I'm hard?"

"Aw, shit," Lana says. "I liked Ted."

"Juliet, do you think I'm hard?" Frankie's elbow bumps the empty glass.

Juliet watches the glass tip over and fall. She takes a deep breath. "No." The glass rolls back and forth on the table. "I remember when you marched in that antiwar demonstration, when you sandbagged for the flood."

"Thanks. I always knew I was a saint." Frankie lifts the ice-filled glass to her cheek and holds its coldness there for a second. Her gaze comes back to them. "Ted said she needed him. Maybe that is love. Dependence. What do you think, Lana, is that love?"

"Love? What do I know about love? I'm a married woman." They laugh.

Frankie says, "At work one of my friends told me that whenever she imagines she's in love she goes horseback riding. Ted didn't think that was funny. He said love was a yearning in the mind, not an itch in the crotch. A yearning in the mind." Frankie lets her head fall against the seat back and closes her eyes. "Maybe I never loved him, maybe I only thought I did. Which is worse? That he never loved me or that I never loved him? Or that I did and that I stopped?" The gray film covers Frankie again, as though she were trapped inside a balloon or a sphere.

Juliet reaches across and gently touches her sister's hand. "It'll get better. You'll forget."

"I don't want to." Frankie opens her eyes. "I don't want him dug out of my mind. Geez, it was good at the beginning."

Juliet says, "Frankie, we're here, honey."

Frankie puts an arm around Lana and leans across toward Juliet to squeeze her hand. Juliet feels how warm her grasp is, how tight. Frankie holds both of them for a minute. Her shoulders relax. She releases them. Her voice goes whispery. "Ted's fiancée, her name is Bonnie Ann Christensen. Bonnie Ann Christensen. That's a pretty name, isn't it?" Frankie's lips make a smile as if she remembers something sweet. The gray balloon webbing falls away, and with Frankie's averted gaze, Juliet thinks she looks like a madonna in a painting, as though she secretly understands everything. "Bonnie put herself through school. She was a cashier in Kroger's. She wanted to be a doctor, but she had a little boy to take care of. Poor Bonnie Ann." She rubs her forehead hard. "I'm going to have such a hangover tomorrow. Look, it's still early. Shall we go to a movie? Or would you rather sit around on the porch?"

"Let's do that," Lana says. "Let's sit on your old porch."

They pay the check, and Frankie thanks the waitress. "Those are pretty earrings," Frankie says. The waitress's small hands flutter up to her face. She smiles at the compliment.

The woman in the pink tank top and the man are leaving the bar. They walk by the booth with the three ladies, and the woman stumbles against a chair leg but he catches her arm. The lady in polka dots anxiously says, "Careful, dear," and pats the hand that the woman used to steady herself on the table. She laughs gratefully, and she and her man continue on their way.

The lady in polka dots goes across the floor to the jukebox and selects a song. It is an old song, about love and tenderness. She glides and shuffles back to the booth, with her arms raised in front of her as if someone were inside her embrace, dancing with her. She hums softly. The other two ladies in the booth sway to the music.

Frankie quietly beats time on the table with her fingers. They wait until the song is over, stand up, walk toward the three ladies who are still sitting there. The lady with the flaring glasses takes them off and has blue, really amazing blue eyes in a tan face. The lady in polka dots waves at Frankie with her crumpled handkerchief in her hand. Frankie pauses at the door and waves back.

They walk slowly up Hill Street toward the bluffs overlooking the Ohio. The river is dark and flat from this distance. Juliet hears a caw and turns to see Frankie watching a bluejay rising on its swoop of wings until it disappears into the dusk. Twilight has fallen and the three women stop to enjoy the moment. Along the horizon glows a thin line of embers, and above that red blends into blue, and blue into black, and black into purple.

I V

Your past will intervene with your future.
– Fortune Cookie

And it seemed that but a little while and the solution would be found
and there would begin a lovely new life; and to both of them it was
perfectly clear that the end was still very far off, and that their hardest
and most difficult period was only just beginning.
– Anton Chekhov, *The Lady with the Toy Dog*

What They Had Left

Kristina Astrauskas was still shivering as she glanced around the art gallery in the Student Center. She unbuttoned her coat to let the trapped cold escape. The gallery was small but not cozy. Situated as it was, between larger rooms at either side, the gallery felt like a passageway. An occasional couple holding hands strolled through, or a group, laughing and shoving, on their way to the movie theater or the listening lounge. The new term had only just begun, so everybody felt they had plenty of time. The jolly blond retreating downstairs might have been in her Freshman Composition class. She had not memorized all her pupils' names yet. They were handsome in their Americanness: even in winter no thick caps or babushkas to confine their full clouds of hair, their self-assured beauty; no gold teeth in their mouths. They were straight-limbed lawyers' kids, innocently commanding and belonging. But even as she thought that she knew it was untrue; plenty of them were farmers' children; plenty of them were squat and sheepish; plenty of them were tongue-tied.

She was the only one examining these paintings shipped from the other side of the world. In the now-quiet, beige-carpeted room she paused for a moment to savor some lukewarm nostalgia, but it would not be summoned.

What she expected was glass cabinets filled with quaint embroidered pillowcases, cross-stitched tablecloths and runners, handwoven sashes and bookmarks, wooden clogs (the Lithuanian word was what?—*klumpiai*), woolen scarves with figures of daisies and roses, amber beads and brooches in the shape of tulips or pine trees. Something was off.

She searched out the advertisement that had come to her campus mailbox: it did indeed say "Painters and Printmakers," not crafts or folk art, and it was indeed the Baltic art exhibit, the last day. She had misread the announcement, misremembered, nearly missed it, proved again the psychologist's proof of subjectivity—what do you see in the picture? An old crone or a beautiful young woman? Yes, they were both there.

This painting by Jonas Ceponis, *Old Country Estate*. Heavy impasto; glossy, saturated colors so vivid there might have been an electric bulb glowing behind the canvas. A burning blue night, a crimson and fierce circle of moon, a slanting red lamppost dividing the picture in half, and on the vanishing point a vague forest beside a vague house. Was it old as in "Old Country" and therefore possibly a new establishment in an old country? Or old as in "old estate," a decaying plantation? She could not tell.

What her parents expected when they landed in America in the exact middle of the twentieth century, 1950, was not exactly streets paved with gold—paving itself was a munificence to farmer peasants from the Old Country, so old it might have been the nineteenth century. "We are strong weeds," her father would lecture, trying to hush his wife in her bewildered homesickness. "We grow anywhere."

They did not understand thermos bottles or acorn squash, and they made peanut butter sandwiches with butter on one slice of bread, so it would slide down your throat, they said. They resented the squeezable white bread of America. After the health fad of the seventies, they were able to buy coarse dark bread. America had gone European. Now, in 1988, her parents avoided butter because of the cholesterol. They had gone American. They had a Sony Trinitron color TV and a Buick, and Kristina made tabouli for them as they clucked and said in mild puzzlement that cracked wheat was what they used to feed to the pigs.

Her mother would become plaintive. "In Lietuva—"

"Forget Lietuva," her father would command. "Boiled pota-toes! Here is America. Here we eat turkey." His eye fixed on his wife, he piled the chunks high on his plate on top of the mashed potatoes and canned cranberry sauce, pouring gravy wastefully over everything, a display of wealth, a leaning tower of Ameri-can turkey.

Another oil on canvas, *Long Distance* by Leonardas Tuleikis, more abstract. Against a brash magenta background, a horizontal band one-third of the way down with flecks of green and orange and yellow. In the foreground three ghostly figures, perhaps spec-tators, with haughty lavender profiles striding away from them. Was *Long Distance* a race? Or was it a longing view from afar?

Feeding of a Horse by Jonas Daniliauskas. Cartoon outlines, the horse's head pale turqoise, sticking out the barn door; a woman at the edge of the painting, just entering the frame; an-other woman, younger, in front of the barn, wearing a green skirt and small blue boots, her hands clasped modestly, with a tiny blue dot of a mouth as if saying, *ho hum* or *it's okay.*

Another painting, lacking the identifying card, but she sup-posed it was Daniliauskas's from his style. Two women in a golden meadow, one in a loose red jacket floating in headfirst from the sky, the other lifting up toward her an untroubled face and black button nose, not anxious, matter-of-fact, very normal, ready to catch her. *I am weightless, I am giddy, watch me fly.*

That morning she had been in an argument with Rita. Rita had forgotten her brand-new Reeboks in the locker room, and when she went back to find them they were gone. Kristina said Rita could pay for the next pair herself. Rita kept whining that she would have to give up movies and popcorn for months. She did not think that was fair.

Kristina had been firm. "When I was thirteen—"

"I don't care what it was like back then!" Rita had shrieked. "I *know* Gramma and Gramps crossed the border. I *know* they were broke and poor and hungry. I *know* they didn't have running shoes. I don't care!" She took the stairs two at a time to her room.

Kristina was not allowed to date until she was eighteen. And she wore old-lady (they were really Girl Scout), lace-up brown shoes in the eighth grade. In some kind of spite against themselves and their adoptive country, her parents promised she would never wear blue jeans—"dungarees" they were called then, work clothes, poor clothes. Now in her Liz Claiborne fifty-dollar denims and Larry Levine jacket, she was indistinguishable from lawyers' wives. She had arrived in America.

She had married a surveyor (mostly roads) for the county, who on one side of his family was squarely D.A.R. (his grandmother had traced her line back to the American Revolution, and the other side was horse thieves, her husband said). Their daughter was intelligent as well as beautiful. May Rita always be happy and healthy.

In Lithuania a gypsy had predicted that her mother would die in her fifty-fifth year. Her mother approached that birthday with a thudding, paralyzing dread. "Here something is not right. My *širde* hurts." Her hand fluttered over her heart, then up to her head aimlessly. "I don't feel finished," she moaned, anxiously twisting her fingers in her hair, patting the stray wisps, tightening the already tight braids.

"Nothing to finish," her father said in his practical, unbelieving tone, waving aside her fearful premonitions. "No worry. Nothing worry."

Her mother was not free of the dread until that year was past.

Now Kristina was beginning to feel arthritis in her knees and elbows, a twinge at the top of her knees. What had been a schematic drawing of socket and ligament in her high school science text was not merely visualized now, but enfleshed, engraved in the bone—her mother's arthritis, a circle of feeble, heated pain. Her mother still wore her hair parted in the center and skinned back into a braided bun at the nape of her neck. You did not have to hear her broken English to know she was an immigrant. In the sixties Kristina had grown her hair long, to her waist, worn a granny dress, gone barefoot in the summer. That was the fashion. A whole generation went pioneer, went peasant. She should write a short story about the flower children, their hope in the future even as they clothed themselves in the past; she should get it down in black and white, or—now with computers—put green on the screen.

Her parents could not read English, ah could not read Lithuanian. That was what her parents had sacrificed: relatives, community, cousins, conversation with their daughter. She would never have given that up—not even for America. There was not ocean enough in all the world to separate her from Rita. What would it be like to talk to Rita in a language of arrested development, of broken English and broken Lithuanian? Unimaginable. Unendurable. Too much would have been broken.

At seventy-three her mother still planted a garden of tomatoes, dill, parsley, and American squash; but roses as well and zinnias—useless beauty, her mother would have said if she were to articulate it.

"You should rest, Mama, relax, not work so hard."

"In the grave I will relax." On her hands and knees, pulling weeds. The morning yard still dewy, shimmering with sunlight, the rich damp smell of opened earth. "Last night I dreamed about you. You were a little girl again, in a yellow field, singing. I was young also. We were in Lietuva." Kristina had been born in the United States, had never been in Lithuania. Squinting against the sun, her mother raised her face from the weeds to her scolding daughter standing over her. From one of her mother's hands dangled an uprooted dandelion. With her other hand, she shaded her eyes and smiled, making a net of wrinkles on her face that was a refutation of youth and Lithuania.

Kristina turned away from the painting. There was Michael Chandler Holm, watching her, confident and placid, waiting for her to notice him. With his sun-bleached hair and broad shoulders he looked like a swimmer but was a runner, missing assignments and cutting classes for track meets. He was not apologetic about late papers. Relaxed, with his straight posture and imposing size, he appeared accustomed to being understood, as he strode up to the front of the room to ask for an extension because the team had competed in Duluth over the weekend or had gone to an awards ceremony in St. Paul. His smile was genuine and his teeth perfect. When he spoke, however, it was softly, tentatively, and almost as if he were drawing in air rather than expelling it in sound. At first she had mistaken his uncertainty for mockery.

They had seen each other about a month ago at a wedding where Michael was the best man for another former student of hers, Ken Downs. Had Michael heard from him?

Michael had just mailed off a talking letter to him.

"An audiocassette?"

"Yes," he said in a tone faint as a breath, in a voice like gauze.

There was a video camera at Ken's wedding. At Kristina's wedding friends snapped color Polaroids. At her parents' wedding in Lithuania just before the war, they took black-and-white photographs, but these were left behind, lost. Her mother told Kristina she had worn black because her father had died the previous month. Her mother continued mourning in her colors— brown, charcoal gray, muddy purple; the gayest color she would wear was blue.

Michael offered hesitantly, "We had dinner with Ken and Janet and some friends a couple days before they flew to England."

Kristina did not go to weddings, did not have relatives here, but she liked Ken and she marveled at his large family and easy camaraderie. She wanted to comprehend that connectedness. The ceremony had taken place in a stylish, restored farmhouse on what had once been the edge of the vast prairie. "How was it? How was the dinner?"

Michael cleared his throat and shifted to his other foot. "Real uncomfortable."

"Why was that?"

"Oh, newlyweds, I guess, you know."

"Was it that the friends of the bride and the groom didn't know each other?" She was probing, presuming on her magisterial relationship to this former student. No right really to keep quizzing him, he had passed out of the course three years ago, but she wanted to know why these smooth people were not comfortable.

"Melinda knew Ken, and Larry knew Janet and, course, I knew Ken and Janet. Toohi was sick and didn't come, but Steve knew Janet. They used to go together." He lowered his eyes. He was not confident, she had been wrong about that. He was not relaxed. "Nobody talked. It was uncomfortable. Ken just sat apart from everyone. The only people who talked all evening were Janet and Steve. He drank too much. They talked about success and how to get it, and money, and how he was moving to California." Michael concentrated on his shoes as if he were trying to be accurate in his recollection, as if it were for posterity or for the court, as if he had failed in that conversation, as if he might himself fail at success. "I expected it to be different than it was. This was the old gang."

His disappointment settled, crystallized, and she was sorry she had raised the question. She put on a brisk cheerfulness to get across the moment. "These paintings are done in an international style. They could have come from San Francisco. I expected something much more folk art, more old-fashioned, maybe geometric patterns. And those over there look like Chagall, don't you think?" Now why did she feel the need to impress him with her sophistication?

He smiled. Was he patronizing or nervous?

She pointed to the wall they faced on which were moody paintings in dark colors. "How do you like those?"

"I like that one." A painting by Dzemma Skulme, a Latvian, *Departure:* a woman in white robes and veil gliding toward a stone gateway that might have been the ruins of an arch. "It's kind of haunting." He tilted his head and narrowed his eyes. "It's a threshold. It depends on how you look at it. I think she's still got a lot left. But it is sad too."

"All of her work is sad. Notice the titles: *Alone, In the Wind, Iphigenia.*" There she was, teaching again, an English teacher teaching art to an art major in, of all places, the Student Center. Change the subject, Kristina. "Why did you switch from English to Art?"

He was silent for a while. "I, well, liked, enjoyed literature—but, see, I felt I never belonged there. . . . I didn't feel I should be there." The soft dust in his voice solidified like ice. "I expected it to be different."

She nodded mechanically, the teacher idly reassuring the student that he was on course, proceeding normally. "And how do you find it there?"

"It's okay." He shrugged, vague and reluctant. "I'm doing good."

"You pleased with the program?"

He patted his hair down, like her mother, she thought. He averted his eyes. "When Cathy and I moved down here from Duluth—well, we were having problems, a new baby, but things got better down here and we're both back in school." He licked his lips. Trying to make something easier to say? "I'm taking Art History 301 now."

"With Alexander Hayden?"

"Yes."

"You learning a lot?" Probing, probing, probing. Nosy, coaxing, trying to place herself among her colleagues. Discover her station in life, her cubbyhole and hiding place. Is Dr. Thomas as snobby as she seems? Is Dr. Purdy that pompous? Is Dr. Campbell ambitious for a deanship? And Dr. Astrauskas, is she that nice? No, she is not. She is not nice. She does not tell you to have a nice day. "How is it? The course?"

"Well, I'm not sure." Stiff, formal, protecting himself. "I get the impression that he doesn't care if the students learn." He took a deep breath. "It's as if he's teaching the students who have had him before. And the rest don't matter."

Now why was she glad to hear that? Did it make her superior to Hayden? Or allies with Michael? "A clique?"

"I feel left out."

He was not confident. This strong-boned, rough-skinned, sleek-moving American boy-man was, after all, disconnected, on edge, a little off. He needed guarding. She made her voice benevolent and maternal. "I enjoyed having you in my class. You loved *The Odyssey*, I could tell. It was fun teaching you."

"Thanks." Whatever was sealed up now unpacked itself. He smiled frankly, his lips stretching the smile far, as far as his gray eyes.

"You were always a very good student." She wanted to comfort him even at the expense of a lie.

He loosened and became contemplative, his eyes settling on something in the distance. "My parents wonder when Cathy and I will get jobs, be grown-ups. Maybe they're right." He gazed across the room to the window in the opposite wall. Outside, the electric billboard in front of the Student Center was blinking, spilling words against the night sky. "Boy, a baby really changes your life." He shook his head and let his breath out sharply but not in resignation or regret, more like amusement and surprise. "We left Duluth and things got better between Cathy and me. And then we moved down here. We left our parents and friends. And Ken's stationed in England." He spoke in a drifting voice. "Our credits transferred. The instructors I've had so far, they don't seem enthusiastic about teaching." Now he became rueful. "We might just as well have stayed up there. Well, we're here. I guess we'll make the best of it."

"It must be difficult for the two of you both in school and with a baby."

"We're doing okay." Sighing faintly and then, pensiveness dissolved, he relaxed into a smile.

They were at the end of the row of paintings and beside a tall window looking out on the plaza. Bells chimed the hour through the clear air.

Outside the window, the evening was pooling in black brilliance, and the electric billboard flashed the temperature and time, flashed out of place as if this were a tanning parlor or as if it were a scoreboard and the home team was losing, flashed TRIVIA GETAWAY, "WHEN A STRANGER CALLS," PICK UP FEE STATEMENTS TUESDAY AT BALLROOM, did not flash this art show.

The deep dusk looked smooth and empty all the way to the stars.

"I expected snow." He checked the clock on the wall. "It's suppertime. I guess I should go home."

"Good luck with your class."

"I'll do all right." He piled his books and tablets together and put them in his canvas knapsack. "How's your writing coming?"

"Fine." She watched him neatly buckle the knapsack, the fingers light and quick, getting ready to leave, now zipping his jacket up. She, too, needed comfort. "Not so fine." She answered the questions that gathered on his face. "Oh, I'm almost at the end of something. It's hard. I need to finish it and get on to something else."

He considered her answer carefully, turning it over, trying to absorb it. He said simply, patiently, "You will." She might have been his child who needed a promise that a bruise would heal, his child on the verge of grief. "You will," he said again.

She wanted more.

"You know, you were one of the best teachers I had." He had been in only that one class of hers, had not taken any others. And yet perhaps he did mean it.

For this instant he was precisely right. She was grateful. "Better go or you'll be late for dinner."

He nodded, his gray eyes sympathetic and knowing. "See you," he said, in that soft whistling voice of his, already standing and walking away. He moved easily, with an athlete's grace. At the end of the gallery, he stopped and, rising on his toes, gave a jaunty, casual salute before he disappeared around the corner.

One Heart

"Men have died from time to time, and
worms have eaten them, but not for love."
As You Like It (IV.i)

Claudia Nelson was hurrying out of her parents' house, with the keys dangling from her hand, when she saw Tommy Sobiecki walking up to the door of the screened-in patio. Past his elbow she glimpsed his dented bicycle propped beside the oak tree they used to climb in grade school. Her hand went up to smooth her eyebrows, which she thought were her best feature.

Tommy, for his part, was glad she had not left yet. Normally diligent, he had skipped his classes and taken the four-hour ride by Greyhound bus from Northfield in southeast Minnesota to his parents' house in St. Cloud in the center of the state to speak to Claudia. They were both nineteen and lovely, showing the complete perfections of that age; they had not lived long enough to make brutal or uncorrectable errors; they were sweet as flowers. Their lives, right now, seemed to hold endless time.

Claudia leaned toward Tommy, listening hard. On his jaw, he had taped over a shaving cut using one of his little brother's Band-Aids with spaceships on it. He wore a gold hoop in his ear. Cool, she thought.

"Knock-knock," he said, full of apprehension.

She slipped into their routine and waited for a joke. "Who's there?"

"Missouri." The inside of his head prickled. He nervously adjusted the guitar strapped to his back.

"Missouri who?"

"Missouri loves company."

She groaned to acknowledge that he had again managed to stump and please her, and she could see his forehead relax. "I'd ask you to come in, but I'm late."

Neither of them moved.

"I tried to stay away." Shifting from foot to foot on the lower step, he opened the screen door. Without the crosshatch of the screen door between them, she dazzled his eyes. But he managed his request: "Don't go out with Josh."

She blinked.

"Never mind how I know." He felt fuzzy and lost; he knew this would take everything he could summon and more because she was wonderful and smart and beautiful and the only daughter of wealthy parents. "I want to be the"—his Adam's apple bobbed as he swallowed—"invader of your heart. I love your pilgrim soul." That last phrase was from the Yeats poem they read in class yesterday. "The whole world is in front of us, don't make a mistake." His need and his clear voice tugged at her.

Claudia just stared. This was *Tommy*, who was her classmate and friend from first grade through high school, who went to Carleton on a scholarship while she left Minnesota for Missouri, for St. Louis University to study art and classics, and now he was at her parents' house asking her for a date . . . No, he was asking for *love* telling her to break her date with Josh, begging her. Tommy, with his tangled hair and baby cheeks and Cupid's bow lips. His urgency astonished her, but a part of her already knew and welcomed it. Behind him, the maple trees had begun to bud now that it was April, and the setting sun flamed in the net of branches. "You can put your guitar down," she said. She had half a mind to listen. Josh would understand if she was late. "Let me just call him. He's visiting his aunt. He gave me a ride up from St. Louis."

"No, don't," Tommy said. Then, startled at his own vehemence, he added, "First, listen to me."

Claudia held the screen door open for him and he stepped

onto the patio, where once she sheltered a kitten that Tommy had found, a striped ball of gray fur that warmly fit her cupped hands. She persuaded her mom to let her keep dear Biff.

Claudia fluffed out her full pink skirt, Tommy wore a Hawaiian shirt with huge blue flowers, which in the artifice of their design and intensity of color are never seen in nature. The lurid flat petals looped, and the fronds overlapped as if to hide or trap a brilliant creature. What if she released its beauty? What if she tamed it? She reached across to put Tommy's hand.

He pulled back. In a moment of piercing clarity he realized she might not be his to cherish. His heart folded in on itself. "I don't want comfort," he said from across an abyss. "I want you."

His face and posture showed he nearly despaired of the possibility, and so she was not frightened but felt the beginnings of understanding and compassion. "Tommy, I'll always be your friend."

He straightened his shoulders. "You'll move to Missouri forever, *I'd* never ask you to do that. If you go with Josh, you'll abandon your books and painting and become a"—he uttered the worst— "a tax lawyer's wife."

"I would not. I'm passionate about sculpture and painting." There was, at this very moment, cadmium yellow under her fingernails. "Josh is extremely interested in the future of the arts and the environment," she said feebly. "What gives you the right to say that?"

"Hopeless love." He took a wild breath. "I was going to say 'undeserving love,' but I deserve love as much as Josh. No, more— my heart is bigger." He actually spoke like this sometimes—formal, even stilted words that would seem pompous to an unfriendly, unloving ear. A year ago, still in high school, he had obsessively thought about inviting her to the prom, but then the class president asked her first. Tommy went to the prom with a group of friends and danced four waltzes with Claudia. Now Tommy gazed at her standing silent and intent in the rosy-gold luster of sunset. She seemed to be studying him, her head tipped to one side, the last of the light etching a gold wire around her hair. He could hear the chirping of birds and, when he glanced off to his right, he saw a pair of robins in the oak tree. "We have two eyes, two hands, one heart," he said. "I give my heart to you."

She thought, for an instant, green ivy could twine around him; he could be Apollo or Dionysus, striding radiant and strong-thighed through pulsing worlds, and the heart-shaped verdure of the leaves would weave around his shoulders, transforming him into a living topiary.

All this passed through her mind in an eyeblink, along the nerve fibers finer than spider webs, chemical impulses in the lightning storm of love. A flash, a jolt to the heart.

Tommy took encouragement from her speechlessness. "I know you can love me, Claudia. I'm loyal. I have a sense of humor." He reached farther. "Longevity, I intend to live to ninety and to take care of you. I will stop time for you." He bent toward her to whisper a secret. "A gypsy fortune-teller advised my grandfather to tell my grandmother a joke every week. But he was distracted one day, and she died in her sleep at the age of eighty, er, eighty-five." Tommy thought Claudia's hair gave off the scent of spring. "I will never be distracted. And if I am distracted—by a sick pet or something—I'll nudge my mind right back to you."

What an amazing avowal, and where, she wondered, were there gypsies in Minnesota?

"I was making that up," he said.

She narrowed her eyes in irritation and turned to walk into the house. "I know," she said over her shoulder. "I'm not that gullible."

Tommy limped after her noisily. "I fell off my bicycle." From his parents' house, he had pedaled three miles with the guitar slung across his back. He wanted to serenade Claudia, but he swerved to avoid hitting a squirrel. He put his hand out when he fell, and now his wrist hurt, and his ribs ached where the handlebar had hit.

He waved his hand to ease the concern he saw rising in her

eyes. "No, not bad. And fortunately my guitar didn't even get dinged." At Carleton last semester, he met a student from Honolulu who taught him some slack-key tunes, and Tommy had intended to play Ray Kāne's "Punahele" for Claudia. It means "favorite." But now he would not be able to play it.

Was Tommy so wise that he knew all about love? Tommy's father, a plumber, was an old existentialist who had read Camus and Voltaire and believed that the universe was meaningless and uncaring. So he chose a lifelong partner for solace. Tommy's mother kept a garden in the summer and in the Minnesota winter filled the house with plants she brought indoors—basil, rosemary, oregano—useful plants but also ornamental ones, philodendron, rubber tree plants, and bonsai trees that required faith in the future. Tommy said he would love Claudia forever. He seemed certain as a siren on a pursuing car. But he had heard in his math class that some infinities were countable, so what did a promise of "forever" really mean? Not the eras of the gods. Not even as the universe lives and dies but only "as long as I live." Which was wonderful enough. And then Tommy, prompted by energy, passion, and his own mistakes, offered his heart. "Let me recite a poem."

She stared at him as if he were a stranger offering her the chalice of her fate. She said reluctantly, "I have to go."

"You look sad." He would perform cartwheels for her. He lifted the guitar off his back and set it against the credenza. He bent at the waist, put his hands flat on the floor, and winced.

"You'll hurt your wrist," she said. "I have to go."

He stood up. "Knock-knock," he blurted.

"Who's there?"

"A little old lady," he said.

"A little old lady who?"

"I didn't know you could yodel." She laughed, and he wanted to make her laugh always. "This is my last chance," he said, and because she looked baffled, he continued. "MaryAnn told me Josh was coming home with you. I thought that if you were introducing him to your parents, if you were that serious, if you were thinking about marriage, I ought to—risk everything. I didn't care if I looked dangerous, or crazy, or maybe foolish."

Before her eyes swirled dots that her optometrist had told her were "floaters," detached cells from the retina, but they made the scene a vision, giving to humble objects haloes and tiaras and luminous clouds. The Steinway in the parlor had an aura, and the philodendron plant spilling down to the Persian carpet, and the branches swaying in the breeze, all feathering outward. "That was brave," she said, wistfully. "And foolish." She saw his shoulders slump inside his flowered shirt. "Oh no," she said. "Please— I *admire* your determination and your—" she tasted the words and squeezed her eyes shut in pleasure "—your resplendent folly."

He understood the words but not what she meant. An engine thrummed in his chest.

"Have you—felt like this for a long time?" she asked, and she knew she was preening a little.

The medieval troubadours sang that love entered through the eyes, but the ancients mentioned only carnal passion and married love—how did the one grow and weave into the other?

It was in his poetry class yesterday that he realized he was in love with her. Dr. Summers was teaching Yeats's "When you are old and grey and full of sleep," and the words drove spikes into his heart. "I think I have always loved you. Even before I was born." He said this sadly, so he sounded both silly and profound. Something burned in his eye and it filled with tears. "This is embarrassing." He rubbed his eye. "I wanted to be macho, and here I am"—he shook his head—"like a baby with a skinned knee. I'm such an idiot." He had never cried in front of a woman who was not his mother or his older sister or his teacher or his baby-sitter, or one of his aunts.

She had never seen a man cry. Odysseus wept on Calypso's island as he longed for home, wife, and son; and King Lear wept when his daughters cast him out on the heath. But those were characters in books. Had her father ever wept? She had never seen that. Perhaps she had been blessed to be in the presence of only lucky men, and lucky women too. Was she the cause of Tommy's tears—or, more accurately, tear? To have such power was . . . alarmingly interesting. She wanted to act responsibly. She must not hurt him. But all she could come up with was what her mother gently said when Claudia spilled ink over her final project for her honors Eco-Feminism class. That was where she met Josh, a junior, with a mustache and well-defined biceps. Now Claudia said to Tommy, "It'll be all right."

He was lost inside himself.

She had a cold vision. She could see herself on her deathbed, a gray-headed old lady with a wedding band scoring the flesh of her finger. Her husband of fifty-three years had died a decade earlier. So: she would die alone. Only in operas did Tristan and Iseult die together.

A shiver went through her. She shook the vision out and away as if it were a wrinkled towel. "Look, I'll make us some tea, if you like. It won't take a minute. We'll both feel better." She led the way to the kitchen.

Tommy did not move. "I've been waiting for you to grow up," he said, all stony seriousness.

"I grew up a long time ago."

"You grew tall."

"You're not so grown-up," she said, knowing she was being argumentative.

His eyes were a soft caramel color, though his mouth was set hard. "I'll wait as long as I can." He stood by the picture window and looked toward the branch—the two robins were gone. "I'm not going to feel this way forever. But until then, I'll wait for you." There was no hint of sarcasm, not the slightest tilt to his lips.

Tommy frightened her with his unambiguous declaration, the promise of almost-eternal love . . . and the promise of its eventual subsiding if it were not reciprocated. She felt woozy, swoony. It was scary . . . and delicious. "You know, I don't really love

Josh," she said. "I'm seeing him because we're friends."

Tommy stared resentfully first at the empty branch, then at her. "You and I are friends. You're not *friends* with Josh. You're *dating* Josh. You like his BMW and dinners at the Chanticleer."

How dare he! "What an ugly thing to say." Her voice took on an edge, perhaps because he was partly right. She strode into the kitchen and filled the kettle with water. The blurred light that seeped through the windows made the kitchen woolly and dark, but she did not flip on the overhead fluorescents.

He slunk in behind her. "I'm sorry. That was not my best self speaking."

In the living room, her parents' clock struck its Westminster chimes.

Biff, his ears perky and his tail happily perpendicular, trotted in, fixed her with a resolute stare, and meowed. She welcomed the distraction. She petted Biff deliberately and got a can of turkey chunks in salt-free gravy from the refrigerator. She busily counted out three forkfuls to empty the can. She scraped the can and rinsed it thoroughly. She carefully tore off the paper wrapper as if it were an envelope bearing a love letter and dropped the can in the recycling bag.

"When are you marrying Josh?"

She spun around to look at Tommy. "That's crazy. We've only just gone out a few times."

"MaryAnn told me he was meeting your parents."

"He is. They're going to Paris for their anniversary. They need someone to take care of Biff and the house for a couple of weeks, and I'll be in summer school. Josh volunteered because he's driving north for a camping trip to study the ecosystems of Alaska."

Now it was clear and Tommy felt like an idiot. Still, he had made his revelation, pledged his troth, and surprised himself.

The phone rang, long and beckoning. She reached toward the wall.

Tommy was listening with all his body. His lips did not move but she heard, *Him or me? Make your choice.*

Tommy straightened up against the window, the last light of
the sun behind him, his shoulders wide as roofbeams. Claudia in-
haled deeply. In her mind he offered her a coronet of blue flowers, and she gave him a hearty cake made of rye and preserved
fruits. She felt benign, adult, magnanimous. It would be easy to
grant his wish, her wish, their wish.

Tommy extended his hand to her. The telephone rang again.
The teakettle whistled. She stepped toward the stove to shut off
the burner. Love always hangs by a thread. When she turned
around, in the diminishing twilight his face had become wavery,
desperately tired, and sad. All the slippery negotiations of a life-
time of love lay before them. The phone stopped ringing. She listened to the gleaming, moist night that whirled outside. Listen to
your heart, her mother had said when Claudia couldn't decide
what to do. A trembling foreknowledge back even in grade
school, it was this that she was moving toward—through air,
through dense water, through mud, through walls of fire if she
had to. This time *she* started: "Knock-knock."

He was puzzled but he knew the next line. "Who's there?"

She could barely hold back her laugh. "Isle of."

"Isle of who?"

"I love you too." She kissed the cheek with the Band-Aid on
it. Against her body, he felt smooth. He fit inside the wheel of her
arms. She squeezed his ribs.

He flinched. A redness flowed in behind his eyes and gradually eased, ratcheting down to merely heat. She turned her face
next to his ear and whispered, "Dearly beloved, we are gathered
here . . ." Her breath tickled his ear. He would be her trouba-
dour; he would protect her against all dangers, all death. He ex-
haled a sigh and it grew into a laugh that curled out of him. It
rippled above them and floated downward into ribbons that
wrapped around them, around their shoulders, hearts, legs,
around their ankles, enclosing them, binding them both. She
hooked her chin on to his shoulder. "You're hurting me," he said.
She loosened but did not release her hold.

Dotted Swiss

The other day in the new Country Foods grocery store, my husband, Barry, asked, "Is that what you'd call dotted swiss?" and I expected some corny joke about moldy Swiss cheese. But no. He gestured across the aisle in the direction of a youngish woman studying a jar of baby food. Below her, in the cart, an infant in a lacy pink blanket bumped its arms and legs to an inaudible song. The mother was reading the label, her forehead taut, but periodically she leaned in toward the baby's dance and smiled back to it. She wore a petal-pink sundress with needle pricks of white.

I was transported back to 1963 when I was sixteen and my mother and I were in Loretta's Fabric Land. She intended to make me a dress for the tenth-grade dance. "Don't worry," she said, "you're so pretty you're sure to get a lot of dances." My mother was herself a pretty woman, but I think she was late getting there, so her good looks almost did not matter.

"You are beautiful and clever," she said. She reached to smooth my hair. "And sparkling," she added with extravagant energy. I barely restrained myself from shaking her hand off. "What is the matter, Frances?"

I made my face a numb mask and shrugged. Around us were indifferent mounds of poplin, sailcloth, cotton, bolts of wash 'n' wear, drip-dry prints, tables of Dacron remnants in neatly rolled, wrapped, and tied bundles, all waiting to be transformed.

She stopped in an aisle of gauzy pastel summer fabrics. She was wearing her black wool coat with the frayed velvet collar. "I'm reminded of a dress my mother bought me," she said dreamily, almost to herself. The chemicals used for finishing the cloth gave off a piercing smell; the air thrummed. "Do you like this?"

I reluctantly followed. I would not let her—or me—off so easily. The fabric she pointed to was flesh-pink with raised flocks. She caressed it; she bunched and squeezed a handful, with its hard white pocks, then released it, watching it, appraising it as it fell.

My older sister was in her freshman year at college, so it was just Mother and me at home. When I was sixteen years old, my mother was thirty-seven, young to be a widow. Only much later, after she had died, and I had a daughter myself, did I come to realize that while my mother cherished me she did not always enjoy me.

"You'll look like a doll, a beautiful doll." She had doused herself in her favorite perfume, Evening in Paris. She spread her fingers over the top of my head lightly and silhouetted my shoulders and torso, as if a halo streamed out from me. "You'll look like an angel."

Her eyes, I thought, fixed on someone else, someone graceful and refined, with straight posture and regal bearing and perfect virtue. "It's ugly," I said.

"I'll make a dress with a Peter Pan collar and a bouffant skirt nipped in at the waist." She was not seeing me but another vision or memory. "It'll show off your small waist."

"My small waist," I moaned. "My big hips. My big feet."

"What does that have to do with your big feet? Just wait a minute, you don't have big feet."

"I do, I do."

"Don't be difficult, Sister." She called me "Sister" when her patience was winding down. She clicked open her pocketbook. "I have to go to work in an hour. We have to get this done." She was a checker at the old A & P, which is now boarded up although you can still see the sign where the letters faded out.

"I don't want the material. I don't want the dress. I don't want the dance."

Her fingertips groomed me possessively. "You'll like it once you're there. You'll see. I won't have you deprived."

"I'll hate it. I already hate it with a passion." This time I did pull away from her protective hands.

She loosened helplessly. I must have been answering more and more loudly. She had worry, fear, love in her eyes, implausible bargains with God and the world. Finally she said, "You don't have to wear the dress if you don't want."

Over by the small floral prints a large woman in a red beret like a pancake puckered her face at me. Here we were and my dear mother was begging me in this public place, and I could only submit. We were haggling and she had won but not directly. It was in an obscure, knotted way, and within all the rites and negotiations of love. "Okay."

She paid seventy-nine cents a yard for three and three-fourths yards; today it would cost five times that. She would work on the dress when she came home from her job at the A & P. The positioning, pinning, cutting out, basting, sewing, and finishing took her twelve-and-a-half hours since she was not a quick seamstress. Those are the countable figures.

I put the dress on and slowly turned around. "How do I look?"

She had an inward, glowing smile. "I remember a time when your father courted me." She leaned her head to one side, wrapped her arms around herself, and swayed to a faraway song as if dancing with an imaginary partner.

I was outside this memory. I thought some shifting vision had washed over her, whereas I was rooted in the palpable world. "How do I look?"

"Quite lovely."

I could see her hands yearning to comb my hair. I said, "I hate it."

"I need to catch my breath." She waved her fingertips over her heart as if the indoor air were hot.

"It's scratchy. It itches under the arms. It practically feels starched." I plucked at the sleeve viciously.

Her tone was steady, rational. Her eyes flicked up and down

bewildered, helpless. "Frances, it does not matter that Chuck is taking Cookie to the dance. Life continues. You should still go and have the best time you're capable of."

"Yeah, right. I know, I know. I'm not a widow or a cripple. I'll forget about this soon. Some other boy will be attracted to me. This isn't the end of the world. I mustn't bury myself." My words were pitching toward hysteria. "Besides, I'm going to college. Chuck will be a grease monkey all his life. I've got my health, which is the most important thing. I should buck up, I have everything to live for. I've got my whole life ahead of me. These are the best years of my . . . life!"

My mother swallowed hard and started to weep. Her shoulders curled in. Desperate, dry sobs heaved out of her mouth. What was grating inside, against her lungs, was her dreams.

She did not usually cry. On the outside she believed in stiffness, regularity, and precision.

I embraced her and tried to atone for my father's cancer, her lack of ease in life. I wanted to cradle her in my arms and calm those flicking, veering eyes. I rubbed her shoulders and back. I hugged her head and kissed her on the crown. Her shoulders stopped shaking.

She won. I went to the dance. She was right, naturally.

She dropped me off on a soft May evening that was stippled with stars. I looked like an angel, she said, in my layers of crisp skirts. My throat was dry; my palms were clammy; the stir in my stomach almost staggered me.

The banner over the door proclaimed the Junior Spring Fete (our dance committee had spelled it "Fate" until the French teacher corrected us), and I slouched to a corner and slumped against the wall. I had half-expected the hall to be transfigured, but even with the brightly colored paper lanterns and crumpled aluminum foil statuary of birds nesting beside tissue paper carnations, it was still our assembly room where we gathered for scolding and pep talks and graduation speeches about the future, the past, memories, love, et cetera, the same old place.

I got asked to dance, once, by Donald Pinkerton Webbe, who was mocked in his nicknames of "Pinky," "Ducky," and "Quacky," and who never managed "Don." I think it was a dare; the other boys must have made fun of him. He walked all the way across the polished boards of the wooden floor and, not even looking at me, asked me in a strangled voice if I wanted to dance. Did I want to dance? "Do you want to dance?"

No, I did not.

I wanted to be home, reading my books, teasing my cat, listening to the Monotones sing "The Book of Love" on the radio. I told him "No." Then I said, "Oh, all right," and danced the one dance.

When I sat down, I watched the center of the dance floor, where Chuck and Cookie were calmly bending toward each other, under the criss crossing crepe paper streamers that fluttered in the breeze from the ceiling fans. They were weightless in the music, buoyant. The song was "Earth Angel." Their faces and forms caught the sheen from the rose light that perfected them.

I forgave my mother for trying so hard to mend all of life's injuries with a party dress. Only as an intention was love unstruggling. And even bungled, it could be sanctified.

These two, for example, holding each other gently, so gently they barely touched, for an instant were outside world and time. They were not straining toward each other with energy and awkwardness; acquiescent and still, they captured each other in a floating arc.

Cookie, serene and without cares, laid her blond head on his shoulder; he put his hand tenderly on her back. My heart hummed with them. She was wearing a pink dotted swiss dress with lace ruffles at the neck and wrists. It fit her beautifully.

Mother never remarried. There was a man who took her out occasionally to a cowboy movie or perhaps a comedy (Doris Day in *Lover Come Back* was one they saw) and brought her home late. His hair was slick and flat against his skull, and he had a thin unfashionable moustache and a guilty look when he faced me.

They were grown-ups, I was not her mother, why did he seem furtive? Why was there that clot of fear in his eyes as if he did not trust me, as if I were the one who had the power over my mother?

I did not then acknowledge that, to his mind, I must have been the keeper of my father's shrine.

She lived another sixteen years. She never did slip and settle into the right spot. After a while she stopped trying, became quiet, and more and more smiled inwardly. When she died it was of something physical of course, her heart condition, but I think of her as dying by going inside.

That fabric was stiff, scratchy, marking the flesh with thin white lines. When we moved out of the house, the dress was given to my younger cousin. I was a little sad, supposing I was losing all of it forever, and I had come to like it though I did not wear it, had come to admire it in an adult, exterior way. According to my logic, adults did not wear dotted swiss. It was for children, flaunting its extravagant skirts and sleeves, heedless of restraint, humility, decorum, temporarily defying gravity and time and other laws of nature; sheer but not soft, angular and clear and stubborn, it did not drape but pressed out from some hard core. This fabric was what I would today, affecting quaintness, call "a fancy." It did not have to earn its keep; it was a luxury, a love, a superfluity.

My husband repeated the question, "Is that dotted swiss?"

The young mother was too young, much younger than my mother when she sewed my dress, although she looked affectionate and smiling, accommodating, careful, loving—all the things any mother should be and my mother was.

"It's too soft. No, that's not dotted swiss."

Acknowledgments

These stories have appeared elsewhere, in slightly (or greatly) different form: "Homework" in *Manoa* (1993); "Nice Girls" in *Whetstone* (1995); "Is This a Stupid Question?" in *Beloit Fiction Journal* (1991); "Last Week" on *The Sound of Writing,* National Public Radio (1995) and the *Rio Grande Review* (2000); "Susan's Week" in *City Pages* (1994) and the *Red Cedar Review* (1997); "Woman in Peril" in *Voices West* (1997); "Listening to Stravinsky" in the *Quarterly* (1987); "Frankie's Story" in the *Oyez Review* (1997); "What They Had Left" in *The Best of Northlight, 1990;* "Dotted Swiss" in *Habersham Review* (1993).

It is a humbling experience to realize how many people I must thank for help in the production of this collection, and yet it is a happy obligation to acknowledge these people in my life. "Lucky girl" my father used to say, and so I am.

There are people at institutions to thank for giving me money and time: the Central Minnesota Arts Board, the Duluth Depot arts organization, the Indiana University Writers' Conference, the Jerome Foundation, the Minnesota State Arts Board, the Sewanee Writers' Conference, and St. Cloud State University.

There are people (teachers or friends, sometimes teachers *and* friends) who over the past few years read primitive, often dreadful, drafts of these stories but were nevertheless able to offer kind comments: Peter Alterman, Adair Augustus, Erik Bundy, Gary Cadwallader, Chris Coffman, Mary Cox, Lillie

147

Martin Fisher, Heather Fowler, Barb Garrett, George Garrett, Marianne Ginger, Wanda and Bill Green, Cynthia Hartwig, Betty Jane Hegerat, Carolyn Holdsworth, Mikhail Iossel, Roy Kesey, Steve Klepetar, Mary La Chapelle, Margot Livesey, Beverly Lucey, Bill Meissner, Cynthia Miller, Bharati Mukherjee, Antonya Nelson, Francine Prose, Pat Rushin, Frances Sherwood, Michael Sigman, Barb Behan Smith, Elsie Susan Teitelbaum, Girija Tropp, Irwin Wingo, and Jacquie Woodruff. You all made my stories better—and if people don't like the stories, I think they should blame you.

My writers' group (Brenda Graves and Ann Grunke) deserves thanks for reading these stories in their many faltering drafts, for providing the attentive listening and engaged sympathy that every writer needs at the beginning. We are what an ideal writers' group should be—smart, funny, well read, convivial, good-looking—though maybe we should also try to do more writing.

My editor (how I love saying that), Eric Braun, read and reread the manuscript with a fresh eye and precise ear. He requested revisions I was surprised I was capable of and uncovered in these stories a linking structure that I had not seen.

Through it all, my husband, Russell Letson, read, edited, and helped me survive countless drafts of the manuscript.

I am fortunate to be so indebted to so many. Lucky girl.

Cezarija Abartis was born in Bollstadt, Germany, of Lithuanian parents. The family emigrated to the United States in 1950. She grew up in Pittsburgh, went to Duquesne University, and earned a Ph.D. at Southern Illinois University-Carbondale. She teaches at St. Cloud State University and lives in Minnesota with her husband.

Photo: Russell Letson